SEÑORA HONEYCOMB

SEÑORA HONEYCOMB

A NOVEL

Translated from the Spanish
by Margaret Sayers Peden

FANNY
BUITRAGO

HarperCollins*Publishers*

FIRST EDITION

Designed by Nina Gaskin

Library of Congress Cataloging-in-Publication Data

Buitrago, Fanny.
    [Señora de la miel. English]
    Señora Honeycomb : a novel / Fanny Buitrago : translated from the Spanish by Margaret Sayers Peden.
        p.   cm.
    ISBN 0-06-017365-3
    I. Peden, Margaret Sayers.   II. Title.
    PQ8180.12.U4S4513   1996
    863—dc20   95-44609

96 97 98 99 00 ❖ / HC 10 9 8 7 6 5 4 3 2 1

for Enrique Grau
a traveler on the same journey

CONTENTS

CONTENTS

WHIMS

It was the kind of delicious whim that strikes pregnant women. All of a sudden, Teodora Vencejos longed to go home to Colombia, back to her town, to her people, to the fevered arms of her husband. And sifting into her memory came insinuating aromas of starched sheets, intertwined bodies, rose water. Ripe medlar fruit and Castilla plums. The simple, familiar aromas of her life. She wanted to start immediately. At least by the end of the month. And not let the extra work she had promised her boss, Dr. Manuel Amiel, hold her back. She felt like springing a wonderful surprise on Don Galaor Ucrós, her husband, and on Demetria and Esmaracola, their daughters. She felt an irresistible urge to go back suddenly, without wasting time and money on telegrams or telephone calls.

"My family doesn't have to come meet me at the airport.

I'm not lame or incapacitated. I can take a taxi, after all," she said, as her long, tapered fingers kneaded dough redolent of vanilla and the zest of lemon.

"A serious mistake." Dr. Amiel shook his head, watching her and smiling. Malicious sparks danced in his tawny eyes. "That plan is highly unsuitable, my darling Teodora."

"Yes, a real surprise." Teodora was shaping the chubby buttocks of a life-sized Cupid, and not paying the least attention to Amiel's words. "It will be like Carnival in October, the celebration will last until dawn. Welcome home! I can already see my neighbors running in and out of the house. And Don Galaor, my husband, wearing his best smile. And Esmaracola and Demetria dressed like little princesses. And dancing and music and singing."

"I have to wonder."

Amiel, at the other end of the counter, was preparing the main course for a special dinner. The ingredients, cleverly arranged, formed a voluptuous, brazen nymph whose breasts were two large jugs filled with prawns and oysters *au vin*, which, he had no doubts, would be devoured with the same gusto as the clams of her sex and underarms, the sliced potatoes baked in garlic butter that made up her appetizing torso, and the veal medallions and caviar that ringed her magnificent face. Guests at the stag party for a publisher of feminist literature would wolf it down to the last bite.

"Why do you say, 'I have to wonder'?" Teodora demanded.

"I like to follow my intuitions. And that's how it came over me, like a delicious whim."

Dr. Manuel Amiel, an affable and considerate boss, licked his mustache with an expression of inarguable preoccupation. An expression Teodora had first noted years before at the border crossing between East and West Berlin, when the police had halted Amiel while he was in possession of a large shipment of edible, mouthwateringly savory bikini underpants and condoms that had the additional virtue of a high-protein content. They were saved by merest chance. The chief customs officer had in mind the conquest of an elusive lieutenant who despised the lingerie available on the Communist side and who, coincidentally and to Amiel's good fortune, was suffering the early stages of anemia.

Now in Madrid, Dr. Amiel's business affairs were not limited to stimulating foodstuffs. Like all financial geniuses, he was constantly tapping new mother lodes in the rich veins of his profession.

"Anything going smoothly is going smoothly," he said. "It's never a good idea to throw a monkey wrench into the gears of routine. Husbands who come home a day earlier than they planned are the ones who find their wives in bed with the fruit seller or the skinny guy from behind the neighborhood bar. But, if you keep to a plan—"

Teodora refused to let him continue. She thrust out her bosom and looked him straight in the eye.

"I have every confidence in my husband, Don Galaor Ucrós. He is a new man, absolutely sincere. He promised me he would change, and he did. I have no complaints about him."

Amiel, who when he was very young had traveled to Paris to study law and finance—to prepare for directing the family fortunes—and while there had succumbed to the charms of a beautiful kitchen maid and himself ended up as a chef, contemplated Teodora sadly. She was beyond hope—foolish as only Teodora could be. Even he took advantage of her innocence and simplicity.

"If you would ever leave that man! You already know I would marry you in the wink of an eye. You are perfection itself, the only woman who lifts me to true creative inspiration. You are the curve made woman. Cylinder, sphere, and cone. With the warmest skin in the whole world!"

Teodora concentrated on her work. She was blushing, despite having heard a thousand and one times his exaggerated praise of her breasts and bombé posterior, accompanied by lascivious details. Measuring with her right hand, she squinted one eye as she modeled the little dickybird that was the frontal glory of the festive Cupid. Firm and rosy, with a cherry on the very tip. The cupid was destined for the young and sophisticated wife of a shipowner, who would lick certain sugary details before the eyes of her depraved—and thirty years older—husband to cock the pistol whose firing pin had been jammed during a previous, stultifying marriage.

"Inspired!" Amiel howled. "That is all an artist needs. True inspiration."

"With me, you have carte blanche. Go on, be inspired!

Touch me if you want. As you know, I've lost a lot of weight to please Don Galaor. And also for the sake of art. Go on . . . go on. You have my permission."

Naked beneath the chef's smock, Teodora spread her legs apart, as Dr. Amiel moved toward her, caressed her thighs, and knelt before her with avid hands.

"I can't understand how you came to be in charge of such a white elephant." Amiel's voice was issuing from beneath her skirt. "I'll bet that stupid Señor Handsome Galaor Ucrós can't measure up to a real woman like you. Am I right?"

Teodora believed it unnecessary to reply to pointless questions. Dr. Manuel Amiel, like everyone else in her hometown, knew everything there was to know about her. And then some. About how and when she had received her priceless responsibility. Her unique assignment. To look after young Galaor, to shield him from care, to be always beside him. To love him without reservation.

She was so absorbed in her memories that she did not even feel the hands and lips of Manuel Amiel worshipping at the font of her life juices.

THE INHERITANCE

When Doña Ramonita Céspedes de Ucrós lay dying, she summoned her goddaughter and commended Galaor, her only son, to her care.

"Look after him, girl, for he will be alone in the world. I am placing him in your hands. He is a perfect son, and handsome, too; there's none can compare to him. Look after him! Do you promise?"

"Yes," Teodora told her godmother. "Yes, Madrina," choking back a sob and clinging to the railing of the bed.

Ensconced among verbena-perfumed pillows and sheets, Doña Ramonita licked her parched lips and drew a deep breath of the fresh air wafting in through the half-open window. There was still enough life in the old girl for her to give Teodora a strong nudge with her elbow.

"Good. But don't even think of aspiring to anything

more. Don't look at him as a man. No. He's beyond your reach. Think of him as a priest, or the king of Rome, or the archangel Michael. To you, he's off-limits. Help him find a good wife, one with favorable financial prospects, an unsullied family name, and a multitude of virtues—a home-loving, hardworking girl."

"Whatever you say, Madrina."

Since Teodora was sobbing so hard that her nose was running, Doña Ramonita thought she had better make sure, and so she ticked off the names of the only women who could possibly interest Galaor. The Barraza, Del Rosal, Baquero, and Arantza girls, all excellent matches. With houses in town and haciendas in cattle country.

"You have that?"

"Yes, Madrina."

Then, after handing over to her goddaughter the savings book, the keys to the house, Galaor's baptismal certificate, and a bundle of textile stocks, she offered an additional lecture.

"Goddaughter, do not listen to any of Baby's soft soap. He may be as sweet as caramel custard, but he is also his father's true son. Like him, Galaor is way too fond of the skirts. And just like his father, Galaor has a great gift for feeling up fannies but no sense at all for numbers and accounts. Keep him at arm's length. Don't let him warm your ears with his whispers—to say nothing of your tookums!"

"Madrina!" Teodora was speechless.

"And keep him away from bad women!"

"I will, Madrina."

Lastly, that lady showed Teodora the secret hiding place under the dining-room floor tiles where she kept her jewel chest. Seventy pieces in gold, silver, jade, and platinum set with rubies and topazes and emeralds and aquamarines. Intended for the legitimate wife of Galaor Ucrós.

"Not even if you're starving. You're not to touch a single earring or chain. You promise me? I've taught you everything I know. You can work."

She also made Teodora promise she would lead Galaor away from carousing and gluttony, the American Bar, billiards, poker, and the women who are much worse than the all-out bad ones. Teodora, who for a long time had said nothing but "Yes, Madrina," and "No, Madrina," felt that in this instance she was obliged to ask.

"Which ones are those, Madrina?"

"The almost respectable ones. The ones who ask for a house and a sewing machine but don't hold out for the veil and celebration and blessing. The ones who produce a passel of children by one man, scare off legitimate sweethearts, and at the ninth hour demand matrimony. Sometimes to avoid dying in sin, and other times to provide their brood with a good name. Keep them away from my Galaor!"

"Whatever you say."

"Ah, thank you, goddaughter. Now I can die in peace."

Then Doña Ramonita Céspedes de Ucrós received the

parish priest, Don Imeldo Villamarín. She confessed her sins in a low voice, was anointed with holy oils, and settled back to die in the arms of her adored sapling. In peace, smiling, and with the assurance that from her bed she would fly straight up to heaven. But Galaor had the drop on her and was already getting drunk, in anticipation, in the American Bar, devoutly bawling and feeling sorry for himself. Tenderly, Teodora Vencejos listened to the last words of her Madrina Ucrós.

"With or without a wake," she said, "you serve my boy a good hot meal. Him at the table, and you in the kitchen. Now, remember! Galaor is not to get anywhere near your bed or that little honey pot of yours. He is a young gentleman, born for music, art, and beauty."

Vain injunctions.

Teodora was so sad, and so busy, that she could not console Galaor or keep an eye on him. Like the burial, the wake and all the visitors ate up every minute of her time. She failed to notice the excessive number of señoritas fluttering around young Ucrós from the minute the coffin breached the main nave of the church. The Arantza girls were there, and the Barrazas, and Baqueros, and the Del Rosals. All of them in the front rows, racked with sobs. Farther back, by the holy-water basin and the niche where Saint Anthony held the baby Jesus, gathered the women the defunct had classified as "nearly respectable." Outside, in the atrium, clad in rigorous mourning, their faces veiled by mantillas, quietly paced two purported "nieces" of Leocadia Payares, a big-mama madam famous for her monumental buttocks (the solace of civic leaders, military men, and accountants) and for a rather modest fortune accumulated from managing a house of ill repute down near the railroad yards.

The burial and the gatherings at the house during the nine days of the novena were very well attended. Why would Teodora take special note of the women? She had to get up at dawn to get everything done. Doña Ramonita had taught her well. Bakeries, ice cream parlors, and restaurants in the city bought her fruitcakes, her sesame cookies, her *galletas de ajonjolí*—flaky cheese pastries with raisins and honey—and her meringues. Just as if her madrina—whom Teodora had helped since she was old enough to think and who at the end did not work at all—were still alive. Every morning she prepared three pots of rice with chicken or shrimp, beat the hot chocolate customary at wakes, cleaned the house, and fed Galaor and laid out his clothes. At dusk, in her sorrow and black dress and stockings, she served the visitors attending the novena. To eat and drink and tell jokes and say flattering things about the dear departed.

In the center of the room, seated beside the upright piano, Galaor Ucrós, dressed in slub linen and two-tone shoes, received condolences. Pale, handsome, with circles under his eyes. And with a distant air that literally subjugated the marriageable girls—of which there was no shortage! Besides the young ladies recommended by Ramona

Céspedes de Ucrós, there were others from neighboring towns and distant cities. All, every woman of them, with the overwhelming desire to console the orphan and, in the process, themselves.

So it went, night after night, all through the nine days of mourning.

Ten, twelve, fifteen girls like rosebuds. Including the Barrazas, the Del Rosals, the Baqueros, and the Arantzas. Firing fulminating glances at one another over the rice with chicken or shrimp, the foamy hot chocolate, the glasses of punch and white rum.

"Such beauty! And me, so alone," Galaor murmured hypocritically, the same to each and every one. "I am sick at heart."

And they, scurrying around to grant his every whim, filling his glass, lightly brushing him with delicate hands.

Sighs, pattering feet, swaying hips and breasts heated the atmosphere to such a white-hot pitch that the vigil petered out by midnight. Couples cast enticing glances at each other; all the gossiping was suspended, all the stories spun in low voices, all the enumerations of the virtues of the dear Ramonita no longer among them ... and everyone slipped out without a good-bye. On air perfumed by tamarind fruit and locust blossoms floated pantings and purrings.

"I can't wait much longer. Hurry!"

At dawn, according to the priest, the sacristan, assorted travel agents, and sleepless old ladies, the town was shaken by unusual quakes. Moans, gasps, snapping garters—Oh, help!—kisses, giggling, nibbling sounds. The temperature topped eighty-six degrees, and on the rooftops cats held their breath even though they were in heat. On patio after patio dogs slavered without barking a single bark.

Pity young maidens! They were sleepwalking, or having nightmares, or dreaming of the shotgun of the Devil himself, or they were rubbing ice between their legs or, if the little button at the heart of things clamored for the impossible, bursting into tears.

Every night Teodora Vencejos collapsed into bed at about one in the morning, then had to get up with the cock's crow. Never during the nine days' mourning, nor afterward, did she suffer from ardor or amorous transport. Nor did she note anything strange around her. Of course, she could not help but notice the proliferation of lush, self-satisfied women in the street, indeed, the whole neighborhood. But what did that have to do with her? She had such a multitude of dreams stored up inside that only the visit of Clavel Quintanilla would finally open her eyes.

YOU AND ME

Lying on the floor of their catering kitchen, Dr. Manuel Amiel contemplated in Teodora Vencejos's ankles the dimensions of his failure. Neither his kisses, his ardent hands, nor his unbounded passion had the power to move her. He felt sorry for himself. He was an artist, yes, that he was. An artist enamored of a statue—and light-years away from Pygmalion's good fortune. His Galatea was not marble, nor plaster, nor cast iron, but beauty made flesh.

"You still do not respond to me?" Dr. Amiel rose to his feet with dignity, accommodating the bulge visible in his trousers. "Why do you turn a deaf ear? Whatever did you see in Galaor Ucrós? That is what I want to know."

"I have told you a thousand times, Doctor."

"I want to hear again." Amiel blew her a kiss to mitigate his latest defeat. A kiss she pretended to ignore.

"It's my destiny." Teodora smiled beatifically. She imagined the coming days, weeks, perhaps months. "How can I give up my Galaor? He is the most handsome of men. And besides, he loves me."

"He is a total wastrel. And he loves your *work*."

Teodora stood in silence. One by one, Amiel was placing ovals of crabmeat on the fingernails of the nymph. He asked: "So you plan to surprise him?"

"Yes, I do."

"If I were you, I would squelch this whim you have to travel. It's only two months until all the Christmas parties. Squelch it, I say! Don't ask for trouble. It's better to let life follow its normal course."

The Cupid, with one eyebrow cocked and lips curved in a smirk, stared at them cheekily. It was sweet, aromatic; it was filled with raisins and candied fruit. As she stroked its little ass, Teodora envied the woman for whom it was intended.

"I've already bought my ticket."

"You can cancel it."

"I've lost thirty pounds. Galaor will be thrilled with my new look. He has a weakness for slim women. Besides that, I'm going to buy some elegant clothes and change my hairdo."

Dr. Amiel stared at her with amazement, as if he had not been witness to the year of sacrifices and horrors Teodora had borne in order to allow herself the luxury of buying size-ten dresses.

"Plump or skinny, no one could make a more delicious mouthful. The problem is that your husband is only interested in women from the waist down, and whether they have a warm oven for fricasseeing bananas in butter."

Teodora did not reply with a scandalized "Oh, Dr. Amiel!" or "Don't say such things, Doctor!" as she usually did. She was radiant, thinking of the vanished pounds and her pending journey. She had an appointment on Saturday at the beauty salon on the corner of Narvaéz and the Plaza Dalí. She wanted curls lifting like wings, a bare neck, and one platinum lock. What a surprise she would have for Galaor.

Amiel brusquely interrupted her rapture.

"Disturbing the status quo is always dangerous. I can see it now. You're headed for disaster!" And he reminded her, "Order is perceptible but does not exist in human nature. If you insist on going to Colombia, notify your family. At least two weeks in advance."

With a fine brush, Teodora added color to the red cheeks of the cherub and pinpointed golden sparks in his pupils. With which his gaze grew even more insolent and brazen.

"What can go wrong? Don Galaor is serious about managing the hotel. It has been some time now since he tired of women and seductions. He gazes only into my eyes, and lives for my letters. Our daughters have told me so."

"Your stepdaughters, dear Teodora."

"They're like my own daughters."

"I thank God they're not." Amiel shot her a soft, moist glance, which despite herself Teodora felt in every pore.

"May we please change the subject?" Teodora turned her face from the doctor's insistent ogling. He, after tasting a celery-and-thyme sauce, arranged the recumbent nymph amidst a garnish of olives and lettuce, all the while licking his black mustache.

And olympically ignored Teodora's request.

"Let us review the points one at a time, my treasure," he said in the professorial tone he used for delivering his lectures and seminars on *Sensorial Cooking* and *Nutrients, Delicacies, and Aphrodisiacs.* "Your stepdaughters would be cold cookies indeed if they didn't love you. They live off your hard work."

"Doctor!"

"Don Galaor Ucrós may be a serious man not given to idleness. *May* be! Even so, the hotel doesn't bring in much money. It barely covers family expenses. And you keep working like a mule. As for 'what can go wrong,' let me jog your memory. You might think of a certain Clavel Quintanilla, and other examples of the female gender—"

"Enough, Doctor!"

"Other examples with family names of elegance and dubious orthography."

Wounded to the quick, Teodora untied the stark white smock lightly starched by the former nursemaid to a marquis who was now the owner of a specialty laundry at the corner of Calle Maiquez and Jorge Juan. Naked, she made her way between the counters of this catering kitchen/classroom and on to the dressing room. She emerged a half hour later, fastening a red belt at the waist of a simple black dress.

"I will be back this afternoon, to attend your five o'clock class. Right now, I'm off to the gym."

Dr. Amiel, whose glasses had slipped down to the tip of his nose, moved toward her like a cat, with deliberately slow steps. He blew into her ear and, gently, very gently, made his last effort to poison her thoughts.

"One day you and I will make incredible love together. Minute after minute, hour after hour, night after night. We are approaching the moment of truth. It won't be long now. And remember, I am your future. I am your destiny. Not that lump of a Galaor Ucrós. Never forget that I have faith. Faith never fails."

"Show a little respect, Doctor."

"One day I am going to make that little bud of yours burst into bloom. And you will feel my stamen right up to your throat."

Teodora left the room without replying to her tormentor and ran downstairs to the ground floor, taking the steps two at a time. She was too nervous to wait for the elevator. She had goose bumps. And dry gums. An intense, exquisite pain was burning beneath her skirt! What poppycock Dr. Amiel could come up with! He was a very strange man. So well mannered, so gallant, but at the same time so hateful.

"No one," she said aloud, taking pleasure from the thought, "No one can compare to Don Galaor Ucrós Céspedes. He is the only man for me. A macho in every way!"

The doctor ran to the open window and shouted at the top of his lungs: "One day you and I will be like Paul and Virginie, Catherine and Heathcliff, Titania and Oberon, Venus and Adonis, Amadis and Oriana, Tristan and Isolde. We will make love as Romeo and Juliet made love, Simón and Manuela, Napoleon and Josephine, Orpheus and Eurydice, Wagner and Cosima, Solomon and the Queen of Sheba, Chirín and Cosroes. We will blaze like David and Bathsheba, Orlando and Angelica, Abelard and Heloise, Hernán and Marina, Rafael and Soledad. One day we will know the uncontainable passion of Scarlett and Rhett, Juan Domingo and Evita, Alfred and Mileva, Richard and Liz, Goyo and Valentina, Arturo and Alicia, Papageno and Papagena. I guarantee it!"

YES, YES, YES, OH, YEEESSSSSS . . .

Clavel Quintanilla was the last person to make a sympathy visit. She came one Sunday at about dusk, as Galaor was sprucing himself up to attend a mass the Arantza sisters were offering for the repose of his mother's soul. Doña Ramonita had been dead now for six months.

Teodora was washing Galaor's white shirts, his cotton undergarments, the handkerchiefs with exquisitely embroidered initials. When she opened the door, she had soapy hands and was wearing a plastic apron over her Sunday dress. Clavel mistook her for a servant. Without so much as a *"Buenas tardes,"* and with an arrogant air, she inquired: "Is Galaor at home? I am his new neighbor, Clavel Quintanilla. I have come to offer my condolences."

Teodora was so exhausted that she had to choke back two

yawns before she could answer. A hesitation the stranger took advantage of to swoop into the house, swaying like a palm tree in the wind. She was wearing deep mourning and no makeup. She gave the appearance of being grief-stricken over Doña Ramonita's death. Her dilated eyes burned with a brilliance Teodora confused with unshed tears. She failed to notice that the black silk clung to pronounced curves or that the deep neckline emphasized rounded breasts, nor did the scent of verbena that drenched the long, ringleted hair raise any suspicion. Teodora had a mountain of dirty clothes in the laundry room and ten plum puddings to bake. Instead, she believed Galaor when, his face contorted with suffering, he told her, "It would be better if you attended the mass in my stead. I don't feel at all well. And I don't want to make a public display of my grief."

Teodora was not quite across the threshold before the door was being slammed shut behind her and locks and bolts shot into place. An electric passion streamed out through the cracks as Galaor Ucrós and Clavel Quintanilla eyed and pawed each other, frenzied, enervated, near the point of shooting sparks. Because theirs was a bedding at first sight. No Cupid's arrows, no preambles, winks, or subterfuge.

Once at church, Teodora may as well have been in limbo. Surrounded by expressions of disdain, delicate moues, finely plucked and arched eyebrows. The elegant but offended Señoritas Arantza did not even deign to nod.

Teodora, in her midheel shoes and proper black-and-white dress, carrying her missal and rosary, knelt with devotion and humility in the last row. She was just in time to whisper, "In the name of the Father and the Son" along with the celebrant, as she breathed in the fragrance of the lilies, the myrrh of the censer, and emanations of cologne and mothballs drifting from petticoats and mantillas.

"Señorita Vencejos!"

The parish priest, Don Imeldo Villamarín, had to shake Teodora back to wakefulness once mass was over. Collapsed in a kneeling position, she was fast asleep.

"May the perpetual light shine for my madrina," she mumbled when she recognized the priest.

"Doña Ramona Céspedes de Ucrós has a place in purgatory," intoned Don Imeldo. "There is no perpetual light there, no splendors, no aurora borealis."

"God forbid." Teodora crossed herself.

"She must atone for the vile acts she committed against you."

"Me? She was a fine godmother to me. She brought me up and watched over me for many years."

"If I were you, I'd pay a call on the notary public. He has documents and properties that belong to you. Get along now! Out! It's time to close up. We priests need our rest, too. And you, my child, don't you ever sleep at night?"

"There's so much to do." Teodora bowed her head. "Galaor needs a lot of looking after, and I'm the one responsible for him. That's how my madrina arranged it."

"You're not responsible for anything," Don Imeldo scolded. "Get out of that house immediately. Before it's too late."

He also said many other things. He talked about respect, truth, free will. But Teodora still had to make puff pastry, simmer the cherry filling, beat egg whites for *merengones*. She would sleep a while if she had time left over.

On the way home she immediately forgot that the priest had said, "Get out of that house!" To her, he seemed a grumpy old man who enjoyed poking his nose into other people's lives. How could she abandon young Galaor? That's the last thing she would do. He was her inheritance. So sensitive and defenseless and handsome . . . All she had to do was think of him and she felt light as air, seraphic, with her thoughts in the blue. On the other hand, when she ran into a certain Manuel Amiel, who was a student in Paris, strange pricklings ran up and down her spine. Burning hands squeezed something in the center of her being. Naturally, that was all a secret. Teodora did not dare admit such sensory ecstasies even to herself.

Fortunately, Manuel Amiel came to town only during vacations.

Absorbed in her thoughts, Teodora ignored all the male stares and compliments rippling in her wake. She would prepare Galaor's dinner before she went back to her chores. Monday would be a long, hard day. She deserved a bite to eat herself.

Oh ... Ah ...
petrified
sobersides
tongue-tied
now half a turn ...

So went the song of Peruchito, the son of Argenis the shopkeeper, as he bounced his ball against a wall.

And all the way round! The boy whirled on his heels, caught the ball in his grubby hands, and stood staring at Teodora, open-mouthed.

"*Hola*, Peruchito."

"Mama! Hurry, Mama!" he screamed, frightened. "Niña Teodora's come back."

Doña Argenis came out of the shop, smiling and breathless, smoothing her skirt. Her lips were red as the floripondio blossom, bee-stung from kissing and nibbling. Behind her came Rufino, her husband, a burly fellow with a ruddy complexion and enormous hands, furtively zipping his fly.

"Niña Teodora ... "

Teodora was a good client at their shop. Argenis and Rufino were both fond of her. She was courteous, considerate, and never asked for credit. Nor did she ever try to leave without paying, as many did.

"Please, please," said Rufino. "Come in, have a drop of rum with us."

"Or a soft drink, if you'd rather." Argenis was smoothing down her tousled hair.

"Thank you, but I'm in a hurry."

"I insist." Rufino glanced at his wife with a worried look.

"I can't."

"Oh, don't go, Niña Teodora." Peruchito grabbed the white-trimmed black ottoman skirt as if he were going to swing from it.

"Don't go? Where am I going?" In her haste, Teodora stumbled, twisted the heel of her sensible shoe, and fell flat on the cracked pavement.

On her back, tiny stones grinding into her elbows, she felt a thousand pins pricking the back of her neck. And strong, painful shudders as she struggled to her feet. She was a sturdy girl, with statuesque extremities, but she let herself be helped inside the shop by the amiable young Peruchito. It was there, seated beside the counter and facing the open door, that she began to get an inkling of the truth. Through the pungent odors filling her nasal cavities—beer, sausage, bran, coffee—filtered strange and barely perceptible vapors from the street outside.

The doors to every house along its length, north to south, were shut tight. The air was filled with hushed soughings, sultry swishings, voluptuous breathiness, and the sounds of docks and boardwalks thudding together, hinges about to burst from door frames, bannisters creaking and chair backs clacking. A kind of cloud floated on the night breeze, light, clinging: the perfume of musk and heated bodies, the must of rumpled sheets and sweaty hair.

Curtains, windowpanes, drapes, shutters, all danced to the rhythm of a concerted swaying. The Cerveras, Rufino and Argenis, enormous and roly-poly, like manatees in the sunshine, were exchanging affectionate tappings and delicate pinchings, waiting for Teodora to open her eyes, accept a glass of rum, and decide to go visit her girlfriends. But did Teodora have girlfriends? They didn't know. Doña Ramonita had brought her up on such a short rein that the poor girl had scarcely ever been out of the kitchen and had gone no further in school than the elementary grades.

Peruchito was still playing with his ball.

> *Oh ... Ah ...*
> *Tongue-tied*
> *whirlpool, whirlwind*
> *half a spin*
> *and all the way round!*

Suddenly, plagued by the mewlings, the sibilant snickers and snortings and snuffings, all the outlandish sounds escaping through the chinks in all the doors, he tossed his ball inside the shop and ran to Teodora, close to tears. Without knowing why, he felt terribly sorry for her, and he was frightened by the changes in his street that had first begun in Galaor Ucrós's house on the night of the wake for his mother. The town had diarrhea of the emotions; everything was going badly, even the mass sponsored by the elegant Señoritas Arantza. Doña Argenis, his mama, had told him: "Do *not* let Teodora go anywhere near that house, Peruchito."

And to her husband: "Don Galaor and La Quintanilla are not even married, as God ordained. They should be ashamed!"

"Come on. Let's go." Peruchito sniveled. "They're doing fireworks tonight. Big displays of castles and sailing ships. Come on! It's fiesta tomorrow, too, and Papa says I can go."

The boy clung to Teodora's legs and cried and sobbed so hard, his face distorted by begging, that Teodora could not deny him. But Peruchito was in such a hurry, and so befuddled, that he took the wrong route. Instead of heading in the direction of the Plaza Mayor, he ran toward the square that was the source of the bizarre noises and the fireworks not shot off with gunpowder.

Teodora followed like a sleepwalker. Dulled, her dress dusty and her stomach rumbling with hunger, she stopped dead—like a wasp mired in a trough of cane syrup—beneath windows rocking as if shaken by an earthquake.

Like an innocent criminal witnessing her own execution, she stood there, clinging to the ironwork, listening to the shudderings, the mumbled sweet nothings, the urgings, the shouting of flesh and moans of ecstasy.

"Galaooorrrr! There, there, yesyes, yes . . . yes . . . oh, yees-ess!"

The boy, clinging to Teodora's legs and behind, said: "They've been playing that funny game all evening. Don Galaor and his visitor. They're playing it in the house next door, too, and the one across the street, and the one kitty-cornered from here. Is it cops and robbers? Or May I? Who knows? Anyway, it's been going on and on. Whatever it is."

EL CHICO

That others would do something for her was a supreme, an uncommon luxury that a year earlier (and thirty pounds heavier) Teodora would never have enjoyed. Nevertheless, in her maturity, she was becoming fond of pampering and intervals of leisure. Especially fond of the privileged hands of Dr. Amiel's masseur. His name was Ingo Svenson, and on his free days he played at being a groom. He smelled of stables, liniment for sprains, mint, and tobacco. He had hands covered with blond fuzz, wide, strong hands that Teodora felt on every twist and turn of her body. Hands that palpated, pounded, and ground, modeling her inch by inch as if she were a clay doll or butter from the churn.

The masseur was her substitute for the caresses she yearned for. And Teodora had to call on all her mental fortitude not to cave in to voluptuousness, to the glory of a gratification no woman on earth had known before her. But the masseur was one of the doctor's protégés, and throughout every session he talked about Amiel without drawing a breath. Amiel was his special idol because he had saved him from eternal solitude and made Ingo his favorite model for the ideal male.

Ingo, a masseur son of a masseuse mother, had been a normal boy until the age of fourteen, when his member began to grow at an inordinate rate. By the time he was twenty-five, no woman could suffer him, and "El Chico" was the terror of all the prostitutes of Stockholm and Amsterdam, who fled from the youth as from the plague. Amiel, who had heard talk about the young Swede and about the problem that made his life a living hell, recalled the case of a woman friend, a classmate during his first year of law school in Paris, a fortyish blonde who had begun to honeysuckle when she was thirteen and who had never, never with any man whatsoever been able to achieve that voyage to the heart of fleshly rapture or be lifted to ecstasy amid canticles of delight.

The blond Griselda admitted Ingo's outlandish Chico, and for the first time in her life she raced unbridled down roads of fire; in the process, her howls awakened two hundred guests in the hotel.

From that time on, a vain Ingo posed naked for Dr. Amiel. El Chico was a loaded cone with a tracery of blue veins that pulsed with their own rhythm and, at the apex, exhibited an apple of coral hue that crazed the blond Griselda and filled her with limitless pride. Ingo and El Chico rejuvenated her, and she, impervious to jealousy, lamented that other women could not garner the benefits of the marvelous phenomenon she welcomed with such gusto in her newly Lilliputian regions.

Teodora, of course, knew El Chico well, by having formed it so many times in dough to adorn cream cakes and fruit muffins. And even though she imagined tiny lips on the tips of Ingo Svenson's powerful fingers, at times she allowed the mammoth object in question to travel up and down her body from tarsus to occiput, because its heat obliterated her neuralgia and backaches. After all, wasn't El Chico just another instrument of the trade? Feeling it imbued her with intense well-being, and the therapy would have been perfect had it not been for Ingo's insistence on constantly reminding her of his benefactor, surprising her with massage techniques invented by Dr. Amiel.

"This one's from the great *jefe*," he announced, as he lay Chico-boy upon her navel to drum her tummy.

If she moaned when he massaged between her thighs, Ingo would place his considerable bulk there and, apologizing, say: "I'm not the doctor, so I cannot enter. You, girl, are wasting time. The doctor can kiss the petals of your daisy and melt its sugar-candy heart." Then, proud of his command of the foreign tongue, he added, "The doctor told me to tell you this."

Teodora felt El Chico throb upon her throat and struggled to make her memory conjure up the handsome face of her lord and master, her inheritance and legitimate husband, Don Galaor Ucrós. The only man whom she could allow to assuage her demented desires. Ah, how the mind betrays us. When she closed her eyelids, the broad, strong, healthy face of Dr. Manuel Amiel imposed itself, amid winks and highly inappropriate comments. The debauched creature! Not in dreams, not at work, not while she was being massaged did his syrupy, underhanded words leave her in peace.

"You are a woman made for love. You deserve better for a husband than a blockhead with a loco cock."

"More respect, please, Doctor," she would reply, when she had the strength to protest.

She was, despite everything, a sensible woman. Always remembering who she was. Wife. Mother. She would never think of betraying her husband with a godless, lawless man. What an idea! Dr. Amiel was not only up to his neck in shady commerce. By chance, just by opening a letter, Teodora had discovered that he had further plans to corrupt countries like China and Poland, places where couples clung to certain modest customs. He wanted to saturate the black market with silk bikinis embroidered with such phrases as *Take me!*, *I'm yours!*, *Blow!*, and *Sip me!* and with sheer stockings adorned with pearly hearts and arrows and garter belts in rainbow colors. Apparently inoffensive articles that, when kissed (as the brochure described in graphic detail) and consumed—because they were comestible—tasted of whiskey and vodka and marijuana and coke and, what's more, produced similar effects. Besides other indecencies Teodora did not even dare repeat to herself.

As she listened to the thundering of bones and cartilage and felt fat dissolving from the backs of her knees, her ankles, back, and waist, she struggled to evoke the white, rosy face of Galaor, with his heavenly blue eyes, his perfect nose, his slightly reddish eyebrows, his honey-colored goatee, and his movie star's hair and mustache, the golden fleece that maddened—well, used to madden—all the girls. But nothing! The memory refused to take form as an image. The mocking face of Dr. Amiel always triumphed. Don Galaor Ucrós slipped away as if he belonged to the past. A forgotten time. As if having given up other women, his reflection had become as elusive as a spirit.

Ingo's voice startled her. Overcome with emotion, he forgot his correct Spanish and, with great satisfaction, said, "You, almost perfect woman. You, beautiful. Oh, Ingo be proud of you."

BLINDMAN'S BUFF

Both the main door and the door from the patio were stoutly bolted. Teodora was tired of beating on them. She passed the rest of the night sitting in the front entryway, frightened by the moans, pantings, ay-ay-ay-ay-ays, and unholy cries issuing from the house and roaring down the street like rockets, cherry bombs, and gunpowder volcanoes. It was a sweltering night. The mosquitoes whined beneath the pale rays of the full moon.

Teodora, hungry and confused, had had no nourishment but the tamarind pop bestowed upon her by Peruchito. The boy had stayed with her until midnight, saddened by her sadness, but also because his own house was locked. Affectionate, talkative, he jumped over to the twisted iron window grilles and tried to peer through the shadows to get a glimpse of the mysterious goings-on that had Don Galaor Ucrós and La Quintanilla in such a lather.

"They're still doing . . . whatever it is," he reported between yawns. "Maybe they're playing blindman's buff. Or hide-and-seek. What's so great about that? I'm sleepy." And in a sudden burst he hopped away on one foot, uninterested in the games played in the dark.

Teodora was so tired that she fell asleep propped against the door frame. Her legs drawn up, her missal in her lap. None of the neighborhood women offered to take her in. The old women, in order not to embarrass her. The married ones because they had been in bed with their husbands since early evening. The old maids—in keeping with proprieties—because they were determined to avoid the unseemly subjects of sheets, thighs, and vulgar "ahs" and "oohs." As for the girls, they never gave a thought to Teodora, they were too busy bawling their eyes out over handsome Galaor's betrayal. And the ladies of the night so despised by Ramonita Céspedes de Ucrós? They were laughing themselves sick at the whole uproar.

As dawn approached, Alí Sufyan, the Turk who owned the dry-goods store, who had no wife and who had not slept a wink all night, waked Teodora with solicitous concern: "Varm coffee for you, blease. And varm breadt. You beauty and barfect girl. One in hundred."

The coffee tasted like heaven. The warm roll, the salty cheese, the scrambled eggs were paradise. Teodora hurt all over. She urgently needed to tinkle, but the house was still closed. And how could she ask the Turk for a favor like that?

Alí Sufyan longed for Teodora, a yearning, hopeless hope, because he had a duty to be true to his faith and marry a girl raised in the land of his elders. She would be beautiful, faithful, a believer. A virgin among virgins. Attentive, silent, submissive. He was ready for her! He had built a house to welcome her. He had, besides, a store, a respectable bank account, and even gringo sheets for her bed.

"I knock down door, blease?" he offered. "Lady deserve all esteem and resstpect."

Teodora could not allow such high-handed solutions. That would be the crowning blow! As if young Galaor didn't have the right to do anything he pleased. Maybe his grief, or just not having Doña Ramonita around (who had spoiled him silly with her dearie dears and sweetie pies), was too much for him. And the visit of Clavel Quintanilla had visibly upset him. Upset him so dramatically that Teodora didn't dream of condemning him.

So, for one week Teodora Vencejos trudged from pillar to post, all around the town of Real del Marqués. She slept in the home of Hada Reales, who worked in the American Bar. Grudgingly, she accepted food at the inn run by Visitación Palomino (also known as the Black Dove). She washed out her clothes at night, one day yes, the next, no. If it rained, she wore clothes lent her by Doña Argenis or Roseta, an apprentice seamstress, and wore underclothes bought on credit in the Turk's dry-goods store. Alí Sufyan—who was in fact Arab—invited her to have coffee with him and was very content with the situation. With moist eyes, a candid smile, and a suspicious fullness in his crotch, he chatted about Teodora with customers who came to buy thread, buttons, and lengths of cloth. "No ones like her!" he asserted in his mangled and musical Spanish. Teodora, he had no doubt, belonged to the group of perfect women described by the Koran. Like Asya bint Muzahim, Pharoah's wife, Khadija, the fortunate wife of Muhammad, and Kulthum, the sister of Moses. Mary, mother of Jesus, he never named. For fear of being misunderstood.

Sufyan's customers were unaware of the existence of the Koran, nor had they ever heard of anyone called Muhammad. All they were interested in was how many pairs of panties and bras Teodora had bought. And whether in batiste, Sanforized cotton, nylon, or—oh, the unthinkable!—silk.

Lourdes Olea, Sufyan's clerk, recounted maliciously that Teodora had bought the "real cheapies." White and lilac cotton, without so much as a flower sprig or a polka dot, with which any remote suspicions about a sinful relationship between Doña Ramonita's goddaughter and Galaor Ucrós were set to rest.

Lourdes, who once during Carnival, silent and hooded, had danced three nights in a row with Galaor, snatched the opportunity when the Turk Alí Sufyan was out of the store to report to curious women customers.

"Natural silk? Teodora Vencejos? Even nylon? Not a chance. The poor creature has buttocks like kettledrums. She wears *large*, and that ass has never wiggled a wiggle in any lace. Gas! Whoooo! Young Ucrós would never think of laying a hand on a bucket of lard like that."

Half envious and half put out, she told everyone that Clavel Quintanilla represented the true danger. She had asked the Turk to order black silk lingerie for her, very skimpy, with delicate lace trim, items sold only in Bogotá, Macao, or San Gregorio Island. Lingerie no honest woman would show herself in, even to her own husband.

"Fancy wear fit for a harlot!" she pronounced.

Meanwhile, despite the counsel of Roseta and the pleas of Doña Argenis, who had learned to love her, Teodora put her reputation on the line every evening, huddled in the doorway of her own house. There, speckled with mosquito bites, she would wait for the doors to open, until Peruchito brought her a bottle of *guanábana*, mango, or tamarind pop. An excuse to accompany her when later she went by Roseta's house. When the night was half gone.

"Poor girl, poor pitiful girl," the neighbor women sighed as they saw her pass by. "How naive can you get?"

It was painful to see Teodora in her borrowed clothes, either too large if they belonged to the monumental Doña Argenis or too tight if they were borrowed from the spindly Roseta. In either case, people twisted their necks and backs to look. And the men! Well, they ran their appreciation up their flagpoles.

No one made any comments, however. No. Most were men without much pretension. Masons, fishermen, peasants, cobblers. And not one had the slightest thought of stepping out of line, not even for a peek. Instead, they collared their wives and whirled them off to bed. Afterward, in any case, the subject of the hour was in the air, tangled in the bedsheets. And the men were the ones who initiated the questions. For example. How had Teodora, a lanky and wormy kid with circles under her eyes, turned into such a wildly beautiful woman? How? Everyone in town knew that Doña Ramonita Céspedes Ucrós, R.I.P., had fed her on white rice, boiled cassava, yams, and black coffee, and only on Sundays and holidays thrown in a little fatback, a rib in her stew, or some fried fish. While Galaor ate the broth of doves, liver extract, chicken and veal, turtle and iguana eggs, shellfish, imported cheeses, and cows' udders, brains, cracklings, and heart.

Nonetheless, the nutrients in the stew and fried fish had worked marvels on Teodora Vencejos. Such was Don Rufino Cervera's opinion when he found her, knees tucked up and hands trembling, sitting on the threshold of sorrow and despair. Eyes unfocused, the yellow cotton dress that belonged to his wife, Argenis, pocketing her hips and clinging to her breasts. It had rained, and Teodora was at the end of her rope, yet she did not want to leave the house with the young man commended to her care by a dying woman still inside.

"That's the last straw," exploded Don Rufino, who was getting nervous from all the honeysuckling going on.

How could he get the girl away from there? No one, *no one*, not even Doña Argenis, had the heart to tell Teodora the truth. Padre Imeldo Villamarín refused to get involved in such an ambiguous situation. And how to tell Teodora that Galaor and Clavel had everything they needed? The truth could kill her. During the daytime hours, while she was filling her orders, baking cakes and *alfajores* and *polvorones* and Greek cookies in borrowed patios and kitchens, the couple called on the services of Asisclo Alandete, a young boy who made his living running errands. They sent him to the inn of Visitación Palomino, the Black Dove, for their daily fare. Visitación, famous for her onion-smothered pork chops, her *mondongo*, her stews of shad and dried beef, her fried meat pies, her coconut rice and mixed grill and fries, took pains to provide for the couple. From Doña Argenis's store, they ordered beer, sparkling wines, and pork and beef sausage. To say nothing of the *esponjosos* and syrupy sweets Asisclo Alandete bought from Teodora herself, supposedly for the mayor or the schoolteachers.

Since Don Rufino knew that with the exception of the sweets and cakes everything was bought on credit—who dared say no to Don Galaor Ucrós?—he began to snoop around, thinking that the longer the couple barricaded themselves against the world, the more danger there was that things would go from bad to worse. If they didn't pay the debts they were running up, poor Teodora would be left to do it, as she was honorable to a fault and unable to deny her godmother's son anything. What to do?

"That's it!" he cried, furious. "This crap's gone far enough! Only Dr. Amiel can help me."

MADRID, MADRID

Calmed by the good offices of Ingo Svenson and the thera-
peutic properties of El Chico, Teodora Vencejos indulged in
a long shower, hot and then cold. Happy, she dressed
quickly and started out toward the Plaza Dalí. It was a brilliant day—the indigo blue recalled her Caribbean skies—
and she felt invigorated. In her red-belted black dress, cele-
brating the missing pounds, she felt as if she were floating,
which could only be a preview of coming happiness.

She still had many gifts to buy. Dresses for Esmaracola
and Demetria. Becoming shirts for her handsome Galaor.
Nougats and quince and pine-nut sweets unknown in her
hometown of Real del Marqués. She was going to comb the
large department stores like Galerías and El Corte Inglés
from top to bottom. In addition to her major presents, she
was looking for bargains and baubles and trinkets for

friends and neighbors, and a missal with gilded edges for Padre Imeldo Villamarín.

This was not the vacation she had dreamed about for years. Not anywhere close to what she had planned. But it was much better than prolonging the time she had to be away from her family. Too much time! Four Christmases.

The year before, Teodora had spent all her savings to plan a lavish vacation. Tickets, traveler's checks, dollars, marks, and pesetas. A princely fortune—stolen from Galaor in the Soledad airport as the family was preparing to board the Avianca airplane that would take them to Madrid, with stopovers in Bogotá and Puerto Rico. Her poor husband! Despite his good looks and elegant manners, he seemed condemned to live forever in that small town on the Atlantic coast of Colombia. As if invisible exit doors were sealed against him. And the poor girls, Esmaracola and Demetria, their daughters. Theirs, even though they were two carbon copies of Clavel Quintanilla, that evil woman who had so soured Teodora's springtime years.

Now Teodora was studying her reflection in an exclusive shop window filled with glittering bracelets and necklaces, opals and diamonds, and evening gowns embroidered with iridescent sequins. She checked her more-than-she-had-dreamed-of slimness, her stunning, high-hipped backside, the hair that fell blackly down her back in a cod-spine braid.

"Hey, beautiful!" whistled a sturdy Madrid type coming

out of a bar with three shots of Sol y Sombra still tickling his gullet.

"Can you spare something for a hungry boy?" pleaded a youngster with large, wild, mint-colored eyes.

Teodora handed him a hundred pesetas as the brandy-fired Madrileño looked on, absorbed, stunned by sudden electric shocks in the area of his groin.

"Thanks, you are beautiful," the boy said as he took the coins.

Teodora proceeded toward a kiosk on Calle Once, to find out whether the number 369 had won. The blind man who sold lottery tickets smiled when he recognized her aroma and told her, yet again, that people who are unlucky in games of chance have good luck in love. She walked on through the crowded sidewalks, followed by the magne-tized man and the boy with the mint-green eyes. Amid young couples wandering in and out of beer parlors, the girls wearing their hair and their skirts short. Wives pushing baby carriages and shopping carts, with the bread for dinner beneath their arm. Elegantly suited executives carrying dark briefcases. Married couples arguing as they plowed full steam ahead. Tourists befuddled by a fabulous, gleaming Madrid. *Madrid.*

Teodora tried to slip past two Gypsy women selling glass beads at the mouth of the Metro. One was tall, with swelling breasts and a dark, handsome face. The other was small, scored with wrinkles, and was smoking a black cheroot.

Both were dressed in shades of red and mauve and yellow.

"Ehhhh, you there," screeched the older one, zeroing in on Teodora with the eyes of a falcon. "Let me see your hand."

"I'm in a hurry, another day."

"She wants to tell your fortune, my beauty," said the younger Gypsy.

"Leave her alone!" The boy of the hundred pesetas sprang to Teodora's defense.

"I'm in a hurry!"

"Who *are* you?" asked the Madrileño who was following her, cutting in front of her. "*Who?*" And with an impulsive move he barely brushed her breasts with one hand. "Tell me, may I feel you?"

Teodora did not know what to do or where to look. The younger Gypsy seized upon her confusion to take her right hand so the older one could observe the deep lines in her palm, as the Gypsy's clawlike fingers closed over a proud mons veneris.

"May I touch you? Just for a second." Without waiting for her answer, the man delicately stroked Teodora's breasts. "I haven't lit my wife's fire for months. But today, if you deem it, it will be like *A Thousand and One Nights* . . . "

Teodora could not find the verbal or physical response to escape this unwanted siege. The mint-eyed boy had retreated in the face of the Gypsy women's aggression.

"Touch my womb. Touch my womb because I am barren. Touch it for me!"

"Señora Honeycomb." The older Gypsy bowed with the respect due a queen. "You are the soul of love and fertility. Allow me to kiss your hands and ask you to . . . touch me, too, and my old bones will not ache so."

"Here! Here! Put your hands here on my torch, Señora Honeycomb," the man begged in a fit of rapture.

Teodora touched the Gypsy's stomach, the man's fly and member, the old woman's bones, and the wild eyes of the boy, who hadn't actually asked for anything at all. Then, as a crowd had begun to gather, she broke free and ran toward Serrano, where the doctor had told her there was a tailor with clever hands and exquisite taste. The Madrileño's jubilant voice rang in her ears: "Tonight, I will light the bonfire of the century for my wife!" Through his delirious cries filtered the insidious voice of her boss, saying: "Madrid is not an androgynous city like so many others. Madrid is a masculine entity, it even begins with the M of *macho*. The milk of life flows through its barrios and streets."

Madrid, it would seem, was in connivance with Manuel Amiel. It was bullying her like a jealous and possessive lover, prepared to envelop her, disorient her, prevent her from leaving. City or macho entity, it would not have its way. For despite the doctor, the incident on Goya, the homage of the Gypsies, the beggar boy, and the man who wanted to boost his wife to paradise in a blaze of pyrotechnics, she would have her trip. This whim would not be squelched! And her hunger for her husband excited every man she passed.

Besides, she had to find some way to placate her dove, a black and rosy-red ringdove, according to the doctor's description. A ringdove that peeped and pleaded for mercy and was, after all, entitled to be petted and fondled. Because it was the ringdove of Teodora Vencejos de Ucrós, married in accordance with all the laws of the land.

No. No! Not even macho Madrid would stop her from finding refuge in the arms of Galaor Ucrós. Nor Doña Ramonita's words on her deathbed: "Don't even think of aspiring to anything more. Don't look at him as a man. He's beyond your reach."

No. No. *No!* Sticks and stones . . . but those or any other words could never harm her. The parish priest of Real del Marqués himself, Don Imeldo, had absolved her of the oath she had sworn to her madrina. It was a memorable and happy occasion she treasured in her heart, just as she had forgotten the miserable years that preceded that day of bliss.

"Hey! You! Move your ass along out of there!" She had nearly been run down by an orchid-colored car driven by a girl with the face of a hysterical rock singer, all flaming red hair and shaved eyebrows.

"Beautiful!" thundered a strong male voice. "What a knockout!" Teodora ran toward the building that housed the boutique. She would have enjoyed walking down Serrano for a while in the autumn warmth. To help maintain the weight loss that had transformed her into a truly pulchritudinous woman. Yes. She wanted a spectacular dress.

"Gorgeous!"

Her black-and-rosy ringdove peeped beneath her tight skirt. Teodora, annoyed, recognized the voice of Dr. Amiel, who had followed her.

"Just be calm," he said as she opened the elegant glass door. "We're almost there. Almost. It won't be long. Be calm."

"Peep, peep," shrilled the wretched bird.

MARIPIPIS

Dr. Amiel had heard the purr of whispers and malicious gossip that had charged the atmosphere of Real del Marqués since the death of Ramonita Ucrós. His opinion of the deceased woman was the same as Don Imeldo Villamarín's, one shared by many of the town's inhabitants. To wit: She did not have God's forgiveness. Purgatory was light punishment for her despotism, cruelty, and avarice. Let her burn in Hell!

So when the Laffaurie sisters requested his aid, Amiel was already alerted. He had set his eyes on Teodora Vencejos from the moment he returned to the country and her silhouette had quickened his pulse. In order to see her, he had increased his visits to his aunties, who lived in a large house crammed with antique furniture, baroque saints, colonial oil paintings, and portraits of their adored nephew.

Second cousins of Doña Ramonita and of equal lineage, the three sisters had never been sullied by debauched husbands or secret lovers. They had protected, with equal zeal, family name, properties, investments, and the gratifying memory of Diosdado (truly "God-given," in their eyes) Ucrós. The three were diabetics, and frugal by nature, but considerate, generous, and intelligent. All during the time their cousin was alive they had religiously bought her sweets and cakes. They wanted to help her through the trial of her desertion, loneliness, and poverty.

Ramonita Ucrós's husband had stayed with her just as long as her inheritance lasted. Diosdado Ucrós decided to decamp one month after the money ran out, faced with the alternatives of becoming a beggar or of coming to his wife's aid.

"Either you help me sell my sweets and cakes or leave the way you came! With your hand out."

Diosdado Ucrós had married a wealthy heiress, not a self-taught pastry cook. Handsome, a much sought-after bachelor, he had been entrapped by Ramonita's dizzying babble about the boundless fortune of the De Céspedes family.

"And what if I refuse?"

"Ha! Ha!" she mocked. "You think someone would want you for your pretty face? You're not the man you were. No girl would give a centavo for you. Married, and dirt poor!"

Ramonita's tongue did her in. Diosdado Ucrós, who in his day could have married any girl and who had—one by one—courted all the most beautiful, was struck by a fit of inspiration. With nothing but the clothes on his back, he went to seek refuge in the home of the Laffaurie sisters. And with them he remained for fifteen years, playing his games of checkers, dominoes, canasta, and twenty-one, and sipping a good Bacardi rum or lordly vodka. When he was drunk, he tended to roll from one bed to another, but without malice or evil thought and with no mention of any kind the following day, to avoid causing jealousy among the sisters. They were all for him, and he was all for them, both at home and during the months of vacation. It was a perfect relationship that after the first year scandalized no one except the abandoned Ramonita Ucrós (née De Céspedes).

This was the relationship that had led the Laffaurie sisters to speed young Amiel off to Europe and to buy him a bachelor apartment in Barranquilla, when he was barely adolescent, when other boys were still tied to the apron strings of their mothers and aunts and godmothers.

A most grateful nephew, the doctor responded to his benefactresses' call. The venerable ladies were fascinated with Don Rufino Cervera's agitation and disturbed by the acrid fumes of sex flowing from the once honest and happy home of their deceased cousin, Ramonita Ucrós.

"Whatever would Diosdado say if he were alive?" The question perturbed the black-clad ladies.

To humor them, Dr. Amiel asked Doña Argenis and Visitación Palomino (a.k.a. the Black Dove) to help by refusing to send food and drink to Don Galaor and Clavel Quintanilla. He made the same request of the proprietors of inns, general stores, liquor shops, and grills, backed up by his reputation as an affluent and sensible man. And in anticipation of the first hint of "And what do we get out of it?" he began dispensing favors. Loans, letters of recommendation for brothers-in-law and down-on-their-luck friends looking for work, and especially and above all, promises to act as godfather.

Since Visitación Palomino was three months pregnant (along with half the married and otherwise initiated girls within a radius of six blocks) and Doña Argenis wanted to have her Peruchito confirmed, both women decided that Amiel would make a first-class godfather—and one not easy to catch. Yes, they would help him. They weren't asking for a thing, they would be happy to cooperate with him. That is, if he promised to stand up in church with their children.

"My pleasure."

The truth of the truth was that Don Galaor already had stacks of IOUs in shops, inns, and liquor stores, even in the stands and stalls of the market. And those people he owed were becoming apprehensive. Speculation was rife. Would Ramona Céspedes de Ucrós's inheritance be enough to cover all her son's squandering and splurging? Was the house mortgaged? Would Teodora pay the debts if Galaor Ucrós declared bankruptcy? As it turned out, Dr. Amiel's skillful negotiations came at just the right time. At least for the industrious.

At the opposite pole, some did not appreciate his meddling.

Real del Marqués was a town that was wild about games of chance, and people had immediately capitalized on the voluntary immurement. Bookies, lottery-ticket sellers, and just plain players were prospering. Everyone was laying bets on how many *maripipis* young Galaor and Clavel Quintanilla were getting off every day. An oilcloth tally board was hung in the American Bar to record the daily score. Schoolboys stuck thumbtacks in calendars and invented a game played with beans and chickpeas. It was no secret that fish and pork rose and fell in price according to the news coming from the Calle de las Camelias and the house of the deceased Ramonita de Ucrós. Errand boys and wagerers positioned themselves in the locust trees and under the overhangs of doorways to note down the quality and the quantity of the honeysuckling: screams, guffaws, and mere heavy breathing rated quite different marks.

The contact between bodies, and the energy displaced, was so electric that cats, dogs, hens, and humans felt their hair rising, quite beyond their control. Keeping count was not an easy task. But Asisclo Alandete, whose livelihood depended on running errands and knowing everything there was to know, made it a point to record the precise data. And every morning he tied a red ribbon to the bars of a window. Two, three, however many were necessary during the course of a day. According to the tone of the event, he added magenta or orange bows. So many that by the time Dr. Amiel resolved to intervene, the house looked like a Christmas tree.

"Enough of this," Dr. Amiel was said to have said.

Not true. Even with their credit suspended, the couple toughed out an additional five weeks in bed, a boon to the betting. Odds now were laid on: How many days could they hold out? What would Teodora Vencejos do when it was over? Was Clavel Quintanilla pregnant?

Five weeks more, and then because the doctor was not going to let his aunts, the Laffaurie sisters, down, and because Don Rufino Cervera was fed up with how long this affair was stringing out, Amiel spoke with his friends in the city utilities and asked them to cut off service to the couple. The passion between them may have been volcanic, blazing like Greek fire, but the water, light, and telephone bills were paid by Teodora.

Five weeks more.

At the end, Clavel Quintanilla opened the front door in the full light of day, crossed the street, and inserted the key into the lock of her own house. She was three months pregnant.

Neither the first nor the last button on her blouse would close. Radiant, quick, she seized a broom and began to sweep out rooms long uninhabited. The neighbors could hear her singing:

> *When someone truly gives,*
> *as I give you my heart,*
> *nothing in this world*
> *can keep us two apart . . . a-pa-art.*

THE TIGRESSES

Several months before, Dr. Amiel had accepted an invitation to go to Berlin. At the request of the Walkyries women's club, he was going to give a course on aphrodisiac hors d'oeuvres. As much as he would have liked to, there was no way he could stay in Madrid to convince Teodora about the inconvenience of her trip to Colombia.

"I strongly disapprove of the idea. You have a contract with me, and there's too much work for you to leave now. If you go, I will have to take on two assistants."

"I'm going, just the same."

"No one is expecting you at home. More like it, the one who's in for a great surprise is you," he said grumpily.

"Your insinuations just slide off my back, Doctor."

Amiel nursed a silence, biting his lips. He didn't know whether it was better to work with assistants he didn't know or to cancel the course that was already shaping up to be a failure. Because even the printing for the recipe booklet was wrong. For the title page he had chosen the design of a couple locked in love, a work of great delicacy in the manner of a Picasso drawing. In her haste, however, Teodora had chosen the wrong illustration. She had sent to the printer a faun with a grotesque grin and a glint in his eye in hot pursuit of a nymph. Disaster! With female audiences, you don't mess around. Dr. Amiel had learned that.

"I am going to insist that you fulfill your contract. Where is the material I taped?"

Teodora had just put the two cassettes in the doctor's leather suitcase, on top of his handkerchiefs and silk shirts. Amiel had filmed videos for each recipe—ingredients, measurements, steps to follow—but the printed directions gave the students the most confidence.

"They're right here, don't worry."

Teodora continued packing his luggage. She was sorry not to be going with him. She loved strolling down the Kürfurstendamm at dusk, when Berlin is alive with young couples and there is a scent of beer and smooth young skin on the air. She liked to order coffee in the Kranzler, all by herself, her thoughts on Don Galaor as she waited for Dr. Amiel. Then after a glass of white wine, they would work until midnight.

She hated to miss the fun. The edginess of the German women after they tasted the celery-and-crab sauces, the pheasant paté, the *platanitos pícaros* cooked with cane syrup and cloves, the hot pickled radishes, the fingers of meat wrapped in mint leaves. The mango and *curuba* and *maracuyá* mousses made from fruit imported directly from the tropics. What a shame! The students would be fighting among themselves to be the one to take Dr. Amiel to *intime* parties, to the sauna and the Jacuzzi, to share generous beds and narrow tubs.

"Come with me, I beg you. Who is going to save me from those women?"

When Teodora was with him, Dr. Amiel emerged relatively unscathed from classes and seminars. The students, all female, although peppering him with yearning glances and brazen words, kept their distance—an honest distance. Once, in Lisbon, a daughter of Lusitania had nipped the maestro's ear. And in Andorra another had chased him across verdant hills and shredded his shirt.

"What will I do without you?"

"It will work out fine. The important thing is an obligation fulfilled."

The rewards of such exhausting efforts arrived in letters and testimonial videos. Secretaries who finally had hooked—with a capital *H*—bosses who had eluded them for years. Wives who succeeded in keeping at home a dedicated soccer fan during the last week of the World Cup. Eternal sweethearts who were successful in stirring the fires in television-and-beer addicts. Women who won out over rivals fifteen years their junior—beautiful girls, with spectacular legs.

Frigid, aspirin-eating women with perpetual headaches, blasted by lovers and husbands, who suddenly learned to give themselves effortlessly, without mental brainwashing. Not one, but two, even three times—with fireworks and rainbows—in a single night. And women who heard music that lay somewhere between heaven and rock, as they screamed at the top of their lungs!

Yes, Dr. Amiel was a maestro. His art reinforced togetherness, attracted passion, stormed the springs of beds and mattresses. He righted downed mainmasts. Ready, aim . . .

Oh, Teodora would have liked to accompany him to Berlin. To throw him into the hands of the thirty members of the Walkyries was like abandoning a lamb in a cage of tigresses. But what could she do? She had a date with a stylist on Calle Narváez to cut her hair, and a tourist-class ticket on Iberia. She would not turn back. Her husband and daughters came first. She thought of Don Galaor as her "husband" because he truly *was* her husband. Legally signed and sealed. And a whole army of Amiels was not equal to one Ucrós.

The doctor seemed to read her thoughts.

"And you insist on cutting your hair?"

"Yes. I want a different look."

"A woman without her hair is only half a woman. You'll be sorry for it."

"I've made up my mind."

"It's your life." He sighed.

LA NEGRITA

The good offices and best intentions of Rufino Cervera, the Laffaurie sisters, and Dr. Amiel finally goaded young Galaor Ucrós into moving into the house of his neighbor Clavel Quintanilla, whose pregnancy was beginning to show. Of Teodora he would hear nothing.

"Don't even speak her name to me!" he said.

He was living in clover, as the saying goes. During the day he went from bed to rocking chair, and from there to the hammock, wearing only undershorts or Bermudas. In between siestas, he read the newspaper, drank something cool, or occasionally tested Clavel's cooking. At night he went to the American Bar or watched television. He seemed to have forgotten even his taste for music.

His desertion made Teodora exceedingly downcast. She

felt as if she had failed Doña Ramonita. It was not in her temperament to fall short in keeping a promise.

"I'm so sorry, Madrina!" she wept before the lighted portrait of the deceased. "It isn't my fault. I don't know what to do to hold him in the bosom of his home."

Soon Galaor tired of La Quintanilla's culinary arts and began to send little notes across the street. As Teodora had the privilege of his kitchen, his laundry, and the rest of his maternal home, for that matter, he believed he had a right to demand food and clean laundry in return. Now, that made Teodora happy! She worked out an arrangement with Asisclo Alandete that saved her the humiliation of crossing the street and knocking at that odious door. (And thus, according to the neighbor women, initiated her own Calvary.) Every day the boy delivered succulent breakfasts, bounteous lunches, and nutritious and mouthwatering dinners. Not on simple bar trays but in gigantic dinner pails. Garnish and side dishes came separately. Fresh bread, salads, loquats and *annonas*, guava, *ñame*, and coconut sweets. Napkins, toothpicks, sorbets, aromatic chamomile and lemon teas. Teodora's one protest was to overlook the coffee. And what did that matter to Galaor Ucrós? He had Clavel Quintanilla—who by now never so much as peeled a garlic, sliced an onion, or fried an egg—to brew his coffee.

And on Fridays, like clockwork, Asisclo delivered immaculate shirts, beautifully ironed pants and jackets, spotless underwear to young Galaor.

Real de Marqués had seen nothing like it since the times of Leda Esquivel. Teodora Vencejos's great-aunt had in her own hands carried food to her legitimate husband, one Beltrán, and his lover, Bertha Peluffo. A couple ensconced in another ominous house down the street (fortunately, razed long ago). The scandal of the neighborhood gossips. And why not!

But Clavel Quintanilla was a thousand times worse than La Peluffo. Two thousand times. She had no modesty at all; she enjoyed exhibiting her condition. She paraded around with hibiscus flowers pinned in her hair—the ones brazen women call "men-grabbers"—her breasts and belly defiant beneath sheer cotton, silk, and embroidered batiste dresses that clung to her curves, her spraddled legs, her protruding navel, the months of her blooming pregnancy, and the vigorously hirsute black sugarbush ogled by every schoolboy in Real del Marqués. A double entendre riddle made the rounds among them:

> I have a friend called La Negrita
> Who screams when I squeeze
>   her trigger.
> Who is it?
> Answer: Galaor Ucrós's blun-
>   derbuss or La Quintanilla's
>   sugarbush.

During those same months, Dr. Manuel Amiel had set up a chain of shops called Caprices and Erotica, to great success. And he called on Teodora for help, placing so many orders with her that she should have been able to hire assistants, oversee the work, and live a life of ease. Pipe dreams! The money was devoured by debts contracted by young Galaor's new demands. In note after note he asked for money for cigarettes, for the barbershop, for billiards, for pocket change, for lottery tickets. More and more frequently he was showing up in the American Bar and Leocadia Payares's house. In addition to which, on Saturdays and Sundays at dusk, dressed to the nines, he stalked the Arantza girls.

There were four of them, one more conceited than the next, each one a prize with considerable financial attractions. Their father, a prominent lawyer, owned several of the houses that bordered the plaza, as well as cattle ranches and large landholdings in rice, cotton, and sorghum. And he had every intention of marrying them well.

Which did Galaor Ucrós prefer?

"To him, one's as good as another," Doña Argenis Cervera commented.

One afternoon (Peruchito was her witness) she had watched Galaor as he wandered around the plaza with a Japanese camera slung over his shoulder. One by one, he stopped to photograph eight houses—each, according to the sharp-as-a-tack lad, owned by Don Pablo Arantza. And when later Doña Argenis asked Galaor why he was so interested in the Arantza girls, he replied virtuously, "Because they are home-loving and hardworking."

An answer that did not satisfy Clavel Quintanilla and

that vexed Dr. Manuel Amiel, who was deeply disturbed by Teodora's frame of mind and her silent suffering. It was common talk that the girl hadn't a centavo to buy a dress or a pair of shoes or to indulge in an occasional frippery or new lipstick. All her strength, her labors, her anxieties were poured into a bottomless well.

And no word of thanks from Galaor Ucrós. At midnight he would leap out of Clavel's window and head off to visit the purported nieces of Leocadia Payares. He would stay there until sunrise—going from whuffing to whumping, lending his attentions even to Leocadia herself. Another early-morning client, the Turk Alí Sufyan, once found him buck naked and sound asleep in the arms of that big mama madam, his face buried between her monumental breasts and his artistic hands clamped between the adipose globes of the enormous buttocks town schoolboys coveted as highly as Clavel Quintanilla's sugarbush. One of Leocadia's pupils, herself asleep, still held Galaor's golden (but dwindling) floret between her lips. Both patroness and employees affirmed that Galaor Ucrós provided them intense happiness, and they would never think of charging him for the privilege. Can a price be put on a sentiment like that?

Dr. Amiel and Alí Sufyan were on the verge of beating up on Galaor Ucrós, gratis, and paying the jail time in return for saving Teodora, when events came to a head with the discovery of Doña Ramonita Ucrós's will, which the notary public and legal counsel Catón Nieto had found among his father-and-predecessor's papers. He announced that it would be read, with Don Imeldo's assistance and with the Laffaurie sisters and Dr. Amiel himself among the special guests.

"*O, freedom, divine treasure,*" Galaor is reported to have said when he received the news (varying only slightly the line of a famous poem).

On the day of the reading Catón Nieto, a lawyer famous for his discretion, had to beat off the crowd that overflowed the side street beside his offices. Clusters of curiosity seekers peered in the windows and hung from the trees. The corridor of his office looked like a fair. A third of the inhabitants of Real del Marqués were present. Regulars of the American Bar, mothers with marriageable daughters, shopkeepers and fry cooks, lottery-ticket sellers and bookies. To say nothing of Clavel Quintanilla, regally pregnant and with airs of a wife and mistress of property.

HONEY

The Gypsy women—diviners, after all—mounted guard at the stairway to a stately building on Narváez, near the Plaza Dalí; that was where, on the fourth floor, the famed stylist Aristarco (real name Isidro) had his salon.

In the main room, decorated with exquisite mirrors, gilded furniture, and thick Moroccan rugs, the stylist was applying a cover-up base to eyes swollen from crying. Three years earlier, jolted by passion, he had forsaken his friend Nico, a furrier and partner in a bar on Calle San Roque, to dispense his affections to Don Felix, a powerful entrepreneur who, in addition to presenting him with a dream of an apartment on La Castellana, took him to the Côte d'Azur in summer, introducing him to his jet-set friends as "my cousin Ari."

An abandoned Nico swore eternal vengeance. Ari's

blood for his, an eye for an eye, a tooth for a tooth. A revenge he carried out with marathon obscene phone calls and sacks of salt thrown in front of the new apartment. Revenge suddenly intensified, after months of calm, upon Ari's defenseless flowers. Ari loved nature! And murderous hands had sprinkled lye and soapsuds on the brilliant red geraniums, the hothouse orchids, the splendid—potted—roses that adorned his elegant unisex salon.

A fateful day! As Aristarco applied his makeup he was crying inside. He was a slender youth with palest skin, chestnut hair combed back into a short ponytail, and languid movements he exaggerated as he walked. Examining himself in the mirror, he chewed on the tail of his mauve shirt to keep from biting his fingernails. A fateful day! Unreal. His favorite clients, Dr. Manuel Amiel and the wife of his masseur, Ingo Svenson, had begged him to find a time for, and grant preferential treatment to, someone named Teodora Vencejos. They both had some peculiar interest in the woman's hair. And they were paying a princely sum for his services.

As if that weren't enough, there were the Gypsies. The daughter of the king was as generous as Amiel and Svenson had been. She arrived amid a swirl of women and children, all making a great uproar, and after handing Ari a wad of pesetas, urged him to cancel his appointments with anyone who wasn't Teodora Vencejos. It was vital that Aristarco devote his time to fulfilling certain favors. In reply to Ari's questions, the Gypsy woman added another fistful of money and stated enigmatically: "She is a honeycomb, this señora. Above a queen."

Women! Gypsies or Spanish, ugly or beautiful, they meant nothing to Ari. He was prepared to despise this Teodora Vencejos without having seen her. Who was this babe? Where did she get off? Not even the duchess of Alba herself caused such a stir when she saw her stylist. What was the source of all the flap over her? Dr. Manuel Amiel wanted all the hair Ari cut; he wanted to braid it and keep it under his pillow. Why? Ari pondered. Griselda, the wife of his masseur, had been more explicit. She wanted a handful of curls she could use to crochet a snood for Chico, Ingo's fabulous tool, as a birthday present. Preferably, hair from the nape of the neck, as it is softer and finer. The gypsies were equally presumptuous. With false humility, they said they would accept any hair left over, to braid rings and talismans. On the other hand, they had other demands. Like the water in which her fingers and toes had soaked during the manicure and pedicure. Also, any damp towels. And if she drank coffee, tea, or white wine, they wanted the dregs from the bottom of the cup or goblet. Strangest of all, they wanted to search the bathroom, if she used it, to see whether she was having her period and had left a used tampon in the wastepaper basket. (It seems that menses rejuvenate the skin and soothe rancorous emotions.)

Yes, oh yes. Aristarco wanted to hate her and hate himself. He wanted to treat her as he would an enemy. Make her feel the superiority of a male not susceptible to feminine charms. He swore not to speak a word to her, to emphasize his aloofness. Nonetheless, when she walked into the salon and, before speaking to him, noticed the roses, Ari began to fall under her spell.

"What happened to them?" she asked. "What did they do to them?"

She was a woman of average stature, with broad shoulders and large hands. Hips barely suggested beneath a saffron yellow dress, legs sheathed in black stockings. Her hair, braided and caught up in a tangle at the nape of her neck, formed a blue black, lemon- and verbena-scented butterfly. She was not spectacularly beautiful, but her eyes were filled with light. And most important: In her way of speaking, of moving, of exhaling the air she breathed, there was a kind of special contact with the world, with life, with people around her.

"They won't die. I promise you they won't."

As if in a dream, Ari watched as with meticulous care and devotion Teodora Vencejos removed the dirt from the plants, cleaned the burnt roots, pinched back dead sections, and replaced each one in its pot. Then watered them tenderly as she lavished consoling phrases on them, as if flowers and leaves were listening to every word.

"I'm ready now," she announced an hour later, although by then Ari had lost his own identity.

Teodora drowsed while Ari shampooed and divided her thick mane into sections. As he touched the wet curls, he felt a strange energy course through his bones, muscles, joints, and fingertips. He felt bursts of flame in his brain and the sting of a whip down the stems of his legs. And when he asked, "How're you doing, beautiful lady?" she sighed deeply, very deeply, and repeated a few "Fines" that shook him to his bone marrow. She must have felt something comparable, because she squirmed voluptuously in the chair, desirable, feline, perhaps affected by his restlessness. She smelled of peaches in syrup. She was nervous, she explained; she had this ravenous ringdove at home.

It made Ari sad to cut the gorgeous hair that fell to her hips. But now Ari, too, wanted his part of the booty, and after all, the hair would grow back. So when Teodora asked for a modern cut with a sexy d.a. or a tapered neck, Ari smiled with an air of masculinity that would have surprised even his own mother. And stunned his forsaken friend Nico or Don Felix, the powerful entrepreneur.

Ari let Teodora talk and talk and talk, soaking up the cadence of her musical voice as he cut her hair—which seemed not to have known a comb—according to the whims and requests of all her sponsors. He reserved for himself a lock that grew from her temple. He still didn't know whether he would keep it over his heart or near his groin. He cut slowly, skillfully, lovingly, and he could feel the roots grow beneath his touch. His own scalp tingled with new energy. He did not have to look in the mirror to know that his incipient bald spot had disappeared. The Gypsies were right! Teodora was a walking kernel of life!

"I want a total change. Something different. A platinum streak over the left temple would be great."

Ari said that he preferred an asymmetrical pageboy cut, without the platinum lock. Her hair was too beautiful to be colored.

"The pageboy will make you infinitely more desirable, light of my life."

The "light of my life" sounded like the banter of a man who wanted to get something going. He gave a few more snips, measured, trimmed the neck, and cut again. Instead of using the hand dryer, Ari placed Teodora beneath a stationary one. He himself would do her nails, a service Dr. Amiel had requested and one that Ari had engaged a reliable assistant to perform. Who was now dispatched with double pay and vague excuses. Ari did not want to share this marvelous day with another man.

When Teodora had gone, blending into the autumn crowd, gliding down Calle Narváez like an odalisque, Ari swept up the very last of the hairs from the floor of the salon. He dried, combed, and knotted each lot separately and wrapped them all in tissue paper. Then he allowed the Gypsy women to bottle the water, check the bathroom, and take turns sitting in the chairs Teodora had occupied during the shampoo, cut, and drying.

Alone now, sitting in the dark salon amid mirrors, brushes, dyes, and polishes, he contemplated the thousand blinking eyes of nocturnal Madrid and its midnight blue–varnished sky. Who was he, really? He had changed under the flashing eyes of Teodora Vencejos. In the shadow of her skin. Simply by touching her. How was that possible? How? he wondered. It was not only withered geraniums, roses, and orchids that were sending out new shoots in the presence of that amazing creature. His new hair gleamed a rich chestnut. Suddenly, he began to think about women. Talk about a fateful day! He was sweating bullets! Even seeing everything that had happened, you still wouldn't believe it. What story could he tell Don Felix to break it off? The apartment on la Castellana was in Ari's name, but would it be honest to keep it? Because from now on, he would never be able to wave a limp wrist, waggle a randy fanny, or slip into bed to please a Nico, a Tuco, or a Paco. Horrible. Fateful! He pictured himself with a wedding ring, an ardent wife, and several children. What to do? He was dazzled with the idea of a flurry of women. It was time to go out and score. He wanted to whoop and yell. Ah, his apartment on La Castellana! Was there some way to keep it? Well, no tears. No. The bar across the street, much better. Some true visions hung out there, actresses, tourists, Madrid beauties. "Who will have me tonight?" he fantasized.

He felt sorry for Don Felix. What would his jet-set friends say?

THE WILL

Curiosity seekers and women with marriageable daughters, avid for the first news, were rewarded for having gotten up at dawn and for having waited so long before the notary and counsel Catón Nieto got down to brass tacks. Dignified, ceremonious, he used a microphone and read with great feeling. As if he wanted to inform the whole town of the last will and testament of the deceased.

Doña Ramona Ucrós, née De Céspedes, bequeathed all her money, linens, jewels, and furniture to her beloved son, Galaor. Except for the tortoiseshell, silver, and mother-of-pearl combs intended for Doña Argenis Cervera as tokens of affection and friendship, the will named no other beneficiary. Not the most insignificant trifle for friend or neighbor. No keepsake or loving words to give witness to other attachments. As if in dictating her last wishes she had deliberately wanted to ignore Teodora Vencejos Arraut.

It was a brief will. No one could believe the measured words of the counselor, the terse clauses, the snubs of the departed.

"A lie! All lies!" Galaor was flabbergasted. "This is a trick. What about the house? And the farm in Carocolí? And the villa in Barranquilla? And the bonds in the Banco del Comercio? And the stock in the Club Campestre?"

"Sponger! Hypocrite! Ingrate!" howled Doña Argenis Cervera, lifting clenched fists to heaven. "She owed me for three years' worth of milk, bread, butter, and eggs. She always found some excuse not to pay. Thank God I never gave her flour on credit!"

The butcher, Don Itertinio Perné, was near cardiac arrest because Doña Ramonita had promised him family jewels in exchange for countless cuts of loin, ribs, and bacon. The seamstress Roseta was struck dumb for hours. And the Turk who owned the dry-goods store, Alí Sufyan, began immediately to draw up a list of creditors, looking about like a Bedouin surrounded by enemy tribes.

Meanwhile, Galaor Ucrós was railing at the lawyer and at Teodora.

"What are you two up to? Are you trying to swindle me? Where's the part about my assets? My mother had a summer house in Puerto Colombia, land along the Sinú River, orchards, milk calves."

The counsel, Catón Nieto, voice unctuous and face foreboding, said that such matters were better discussed in private and it was not advisable to air them in public. Galaor Ucrós insisted. Catón Nieto showed signs of leaving his office. Galaor grabbed him around the neck. If Padre Imeldo Villamarín had not intervened, Galaor would have strangled him.

"You want the truth? Well, you asked for it!" the victim yowled as he straightened his tie.

And he laid out all the things Padre Imeldo had tried to tell Teodora by repeatedly asking her to go see the notary. Doña Ramonita had tied the priest's tongue under the sanctity of the confessional, and he, Catón Nieto, *fils*, was barely beginning to make sense of all the papers in the files of Catón Nieto, *père*. Nevertheless, the house, the haciendas, the farms, the land, the stocks and bonds, the cattle, and all other effects belonged to Teodora Vencejos Arraut.

"What! That can't be! Im-*pos*-sible!" Galaor could not believe his ears.

"It's true," Padre Imeldo confirmed.

And the counselor continued.

Don Martiniano Vencejos, as he sensed his approaching death, had put his affairs in meticulous order. And to Doña Ramona Ucrós (née De Céspedes), the bosom friend of his deceased wife, he had commended the care of his only daughter, Teodora. The interest from her inherited wealth should provide for an excellent education. She was to attend the best school in the country, and take English, French, music, and swimming. When she completed her secondary studies, she was to be sent to a university in France, Belgium, or the United States, according to the career she had chosen. In addition, there would be enough money for Doña Ramonita and her son, Galaor, to live very comfortably without damaging Teodora's interests. Don Martiniano had had blind confidence in the rightness of his choice, and he died in peace with regard to the fate and future of his heir.

"No . . . ooo . . . oo." Galaor's eyes clouded as he fell, in a swoon, into the devoted arms of the Arantza sisters.

No one present could get a word out. There were dry throats and slack jaws. Clavel Quintanilla, belly auguring the birth of a boy, suffered vertigo and palpitations. The purported nieces, squeezed into new dresses bought for the occasion, could feel coccyges crunching. The way the world turns! And as Padre Imeldo Villamarín would say, for once the words of the Gospel were prophetic: And the last shall be first. The beggar Lazarus going before the rich man Epulon. Blessed are the meek.

To everyone's wonderment, the Teodora Vencejos whom Ramona Ucrós had banished to the kitchen and raised like a poor relative was an heiress. A princess incognito, a Cinderella snatched from the hearth, a Sleeping Beauty awakened with a kiss.

Neither counselor Catón Nieto, *fils*, nor Don Imeldo knew whether old lady Ucrós had gotten her hands on the jewels and other personal property that rightfully belonged to Teodora. But as for income from the money—she had sopped up the last peso! And they had been able to do nothing about it. Don Martiniano Vencejos had been struck down by a cerebral hemorrhage before he signed the document naming the parish priest and the Catóns *père* and *fils* to form a trust charged with periodically checking to see that his testamentary dispositions were carried out.

Happily, Ramona Ucrós had not been able to touch the capital. Not even Teodora herself could sell houses or haciendas, except under exceptional circumstances. And then the bank would reinvest half of the income, according to law, fortunately!

Irate and humiliated, Galaor Ucrós De Céspedes pounced on the documents that named him heir to a respectable fortune. Doña Ramonita, treacherously, with premeditation, had saved and increased her own wealth at her goddaughter's expense. The confectionery shop was a front to justify her earnings before the town; finally, though, "her beloved son," as he was called in the will, could live from the income—and well, at that.

"I've been had!" he roared.

He left without listening to any further discussion, like an Orestes in a slub-linen suit and leather loafers whom destiny had robbed of the opportunity to throttle Doña Ramonita. None of the Arantza girls or the Rosals, not Clavel Quintanilla, not even the purported nieces, merited a second glance. That very night saw him in the Hotel del Prado, surrounded by elegant women, inviting acquaintances and strangers alike to join him in a glass of champagne.

"At last Teodora will be free," Dr. Amiel prophesied.

At Padre Imeldo's request, Amiel drove Teodora home in his late-model automobile. He longed to stroke her hair, cosset her a little, tell her that life was hers. She had the world at her feet! Love and happiness were going to smile down on her.

Naive. That was Dr. Manuel Amiel. Naive. Despite all his travels, education, good family name. He was short on that last sense called intuition. Before he had intended, he found himself swamping Teodora with a torrent of words and desires he had not until then wanted to confess.

Despite himself, he told her he was falling madly in love with her. The very sound of the name Teodora left a bitter-sweet flavor on his taste buds, tickled his flanks and kidneys, made him feel he was the bull that kidnapped Europa and had his way with her as he bellowed on the beaches of the night. Other times, he was the swan between Leda's legs. Also a hummingbird that streaked down on the banners of the wind to possess a winged Teodora. He saw himself as a triumphantly erect, larger-than-life Priapus, caressed by females of five continents. Women who suddenly were transformed into his one, his only, desired love—Teodora Vencejos.

"You hear what I'm saying?"

"Huh? Forgive me, Doctor. I'm just so tired." Between her unremitting fatigue and her worry over Galaor, Teodora had heard absolutely nothing.

A KING

There was great excitement in the Barajas airport. Teodora had to fight her way to the Iberia counter, so great was the swarm of journalists packed among the gringos, Germans, South Americans, and Japanese sadly taking their leave of the most delightful capital in Europe.

What was all the fuss? Teodora discovered the answer when she mistakenly wandered into the wrong waiting room. Among the passengers just arrived from Romania was one Salustio Grimaldo, the coffee and sugarcane king who also had holdings in the petroleum and gold-mining industries. Grimaldo had spent five years in a long pilgrimage from one doctor to another, because from so many years of sampling coffee, tasting the virtues of various sugars, smelling petroleum, and biting gold, his appetite was irreparably lost.

"Poor baby," Teodora murmured when she saw him.

Grimaldo, who was six foot three but weighed less than a hundred and ten pounds, was shivering despite being wrapped in a heavy shawl, listening while his latest wife, a stunning Caribbean beauty, verbally flogged him in front of the solid wall of journalists. The magnate's unexpected decision to travel to Colombia to undergo a treatment using live duck cells had irritated the woman to the point of this vicious attack.

"No, absolutely no! I am *not* leaving Madrid. I'm sick and tired of living with a bag of bones and of always eating alone. As for me, cookie, I'm leaving! Find someone else to put up with you. Either we stay in Spain or I'm asking for a divorce!"

Her irritation intensified when she spied Teodora, whose large eyes, fixed on Grimaldo, expressed infinite compassion. She shrieked: "And who are you? Go away!"

Teodora, who for so many years had been treated like a poor cousin, was very sensitive to insolence. And so could not allow a grown man to be treated like a piece of garbage, especially with busybodies hanging on every word. Ignoring the wife, she walked over to Grimaldo, took one of his skeletal hands, and kissed it lovingly.

"Who are you?" a reporter from *Hola* asked, and began snapping photos of her.

Teodora winked at the magnate and replied: "I'm his friend. I'm accompanying him to Colombia."

In her elegant tailored suit, kid shoes and handbag, her opaque stockings and exquisite asymmetrical hairdo, she was a fabulous stranger even to herself. That morning, after bathing in water scented with cinammon concentrate, she had rubbed onto the sinuosities of her body several essences created by Dr. Amiel. Peach, verbena, pommerose. She wanted to impress Galaor from the very first instant. Owing to the length of the flight, she could not be overly zealous with her makeup. Or decorate her nipples, navel, and knees with red and blue lotus flowers. In her purse, however, she carried a flask of Aflame, the exquisite love emollient created by Amiel, which contained, among other ingredients, essence of tuberose, Egyptian geranium, Cape jasmine, ginseng, rock candy, camphor, palm oil, aloe vera, opium extract, musk, and a cognac aged for fifteen years, along with oils and jellies derived from petroleum and carbon. Aflame was all the vogue among European lovers because it was icy in summer and fiery in winter. Couples rubbed it over each other's naked body, lighted a match, and for brief instants blazed without burning in the bonfire of love, amid a halo of blue flames and red crests. Of secret and exclusive manufacture, promoted as the prelude to ecstasy, Aflame was a perfect compound whose sales were further enriching Dr. Amiel's coffers.

The news photographers took a series of shots of Grimaldo and his new conquest. Appreciative whistles sprang up around them. Teodora, for the first time in her life, smiled bewitchingly at the cameras and at a man other than Galaor Ucrós. She was thrilled by the insinuating, even cheeky stares of the other passengers, and indulgently ignored the insults thrown by Señora Grimaldo, who was threatening to sue her for adultery, and the heavy-handed flirting of a gigantic redheaded woman in cowboy boots.

"Welcome aboard," said the Iberia stewardess.

Inside the airplane, with Grimaldo's head on her shoulder, Teodora enjoyed her first rest in months. Ever guided by Dr. Amiel's moral values, she had succeeded in getting the coffee king and his bodyguards to sit with her in the smoking section.

"Traveling in Nonsmoking is counterproductive," Amiel always said. "There's no tobacco smoke or odor there, but it's filled with nuns, mothers with small children, and bad-tempered old ladies. We run the risk of breathing wet diapers, talcum, and kid's poop."

"I like children," Teodora would sigh.

"Children are beautiful when they're yours. But much better to fly in the smoking section. It's so reduced that soon it won't exist at all. After promoting cigarettes around the world, now the gringos feel bad for having done it. They charge tobacco with being the cause of terrible diseases. Soon they'll be lynching smokers. Take my word for it. Let's hope that making love doesn't go down the same road."

Salustio Grimaldo was reading the day's paper. Teodora

was terrified by an absolutely hair-raising article about AIDS. She remembered her boss's words. "The enemies of pleasure, love, and freedom have created this laboratory disease to check—what is in their lights—debauchery. The way things are going in the world, everyone is going to end up making babies in test tubes. Make love? Forget it! They'll be implanting fertilized eggs in germ-free uteruses, and the globe will become a truly antiseptic place. No tobacco and no love. Pray God that future governments don't outlaw wine."

"Are you having dinner?" the stewardess asked Teodora and Grimaldo.

Teodora accepted, delighted. She was hungry. Like a spoiled child, the magnate turned up his nose and said he would just have his vitamins, but Teodora was firm. She removed the cellophane covering the potato salad, shrimp, and ham and opened the wine. She tore off a corner of bread, spread it thickly with butter, as she tempted Grimaldo, describing the aromas from the oven and the skillful hands of the beautiful girls who baked the bread. Then, as she ate, she sighed that the shrimp were supreme, and that they had a delicious garlic-and-parsley sauce with a slight hint of dill and vineyards and Mediterranean shores. And the ham. Ah, the ham! It was a marvel, the speciality of Catalonian peasants, cured according to age-old recipes and cooked by the world's best chefs.

"Take a little bite for Mama," she said, because she had

glimpsed the neglected child dormant in the six-foot-three body, the infant born in a cradle of gold but raised under strict rules, never allowed to play with his own poopoo when he was a baby, or dabble in water and clay.

"Take a bite. If you eat everything, I'll give you a prize."

"Anything I want?"

"Anything you want."

"You promise?"

"I give you my word."

Salustio Grimaldo ate his first complete meal in five years, feeling with each bite that he was recovering his sense of taste and smell. As dessert, he wanted to sample Teodora's breasts, to see whether they were salty or sweet, and if possible, to sleep with his face plastered against them. And also, he didn't dare say it, he felt as bashful as a teenager, but if she would let him explore beneath her skirt, maybe he could catch a whiff of Camembert cheese or mandarin orange . . . and find out whether her juices were thick or thin? Could he . . . Yes?

Teodora had promised. And to reinforce her "yes," she asked for the stewardess to bring them a double blanket. Grimaldo, still shivering, buried his face in her soft bosom and slowly, oh so slowly, began to suck, while in the dark the rest of the passengers were watching an action film. The fingers of his left hand crept into the throat of the starving ringdove.

They both slept deeply, Teodora from exhaustion, and he, depleted by conflicting emotions.

Teodora saw herself, naked, floating on a mirror of water. A strong, muscular man, skin brown from the sun, face hidden by a mask of gold, galloped upon her body. Again and again, again and again!, she felt the thrust of a harpoon of magnetic flesh tipped with bulbous amethyst. She was burning, disintegrating, yet intact in a blaze of fluorescence that seemed to have no beginning or end.

"It's him, it's him!" she exclaimed in a glorious revelation.

It was the one and only man in her life. Young Galaor. Handsome, elegant, irreplaceable. Her inheritance, her purpose, her reason for being. With just the mention of that name, Galaor, her desire had been fulfilled—and her cotton panties saturated; she was loved, day after day after day. Galaor Ucrós, the man who one Sunday had taken her to the municipal court to make her his wife.

"My love," she mumbled.

Without abandoning the fortress, still firm between her legs, that athlete with the marvelous muscles slowly removed his mask. Teodora, trembling and amazed, met mocking eyes. Dr. Amiel was whispering, wickedly, "I told you that one day my cock would crow deep inside you."

She awakened as if she had a block of ice over her heart and whipped cream in the beak of her dove. Her ears were ringing. The stewardess was handing out warm towels. Outside, it was growing light. The coffee and sugarcane king kissed her with a jubilant "Good morning!"

In the aisle, a little boy in green pajamas was staring open-mouthed at Teodora, pinching her legs. His mother called, "Miguelito, Mi-gue!" from the No Smoking section. The bodyguards took their place in the line to the bathroom. Across the aisle, beneath a cover, a very young couple was moving arms and legs with slow sensuality, indifferent to the stewardesses. Their breathing, strained from trying to be discreet, yet charged with pleasure, made even the hair in Teodora's armpits stand on end.

"What time is breakfast?" Grimaldo asked. "I'm hissing with hunger." And he whispered in Teodora's ear, "Last night ... ah, what a night! Tell me, what is your name? I must know it, I must know absolutely everything about you."

He was no longer shivering. Despite its yellowish cast, his skin had a ruddy glow. And his eyes sparkled. Possessively, he grasped Teodora's hands as if he wanted to crush them.

"What *is* your name?"

Teodora did not lie about her origins, name, or residence. She told the truth. She was married. She was going home, to spend a long, a very long, time with her husband and daughters.

"You're not coming with me?"

"I can't."

Not even Teodora's desertion could diminish the powerful forces bubbling inside Salustio Grimaldo. The treatment with live cells became redundant, and the only reason he would continue his trip was to be with her.

"If you want, we could stay in Puerto Rico and talk about our divorces."

Teodora looked out the small window. The cloudless sky was divided. One half was a glowing red-and-gold plain, the other, a violet blue sea, the most beautiful she had seen for many years. In a certain way, the two faces of love. Teodora stood up to stretch her legs. She wanted to pee. At least for the time being, she was satisfied.

BLOND BLOND

After the events at the notary's office, Clavel Quintanilla, out of pure rage, began screaming, and her water broke prematurely. Since her contractions were coming regularly and she expected to give birth to a Herculean baby boy, or twins, several idle, husky youths whisked her off to a renowned clinic, which turned out to be a rather expensive choice. Meanwhile, Galaor Ucrós was abandoning the house that since the time he was a boy he had thought was his. He stayed long enough to pack his suitcases and to accuse Teodora of being a crook and a thief and below contempt.

"I'll die first. I never want to see you again!"

As he left, he slammed every door behind him. He went across the street to pick up his manicure kit and then hailed a taxi. The driver, Higinio Lopera, as was only right, told him the news. Clavel Quintanilla had just given him a baby girl.

Galaor Ucrós, an ingrate if ever there was one, according to Higinio, protested: "That woman isn't my wife. I'm a bachelor and without obligations."

Even so, he visited Clavel in the clinic, signed the documents for her expenses, and even put down a modest advance, although he didn't register the infant as his. And *Adiós Clavel!* Don't expect to see me again!

After three months, the board of the establishment allowed La Quintanilla to leave, to prevent her by now quite excessive account from continuing to climb. Bill collectors were already camped outside Teodora's house.

"Don't even think of paying," admonished Doña Argenis.

"I'm not crazy."

But Teodora could not bear the black-clad men carrying attaché cases that shouted Delinquent Debtor, the banging on her door, the shame. She accepted responsibility for paying the debt and the interest, down to the last centavo. An opportunity which Dr. Amiel seized to offer Teodora work in his enterprises, for her debts exceeded the immediate possibilities of her inheritance.

And that was how Teodora came to abandon making cakes and cookies and *esponjados* and floating islands in her home to become Amiel's assistant. It was not only the money that interested her. She wanted to work in Barranquilla in order to locate young Galaor, whose threat still resonated in her mind: "I never want to see you again!"

Where could he be? In what part of the city?

Teodora, of course, would not hear the malicious gossip circulating about a flashy individual on the Atlantic Coast whose name just happened to be Galaor. The same? Her Galaor? She didn't believe it. No. The man living like Croesus in the best hotels in Cartagena, Santa Marta, and Barranquilla itself was some handsome foreigner. He drove around in a magenta convertible, captivating the most celebrated women in the Caribbean: singers, models, beauty queens. They were all mad for him. They called him Valentino, Golden Rod, The Lance, and The Arrow. He was so handsome—reported the other girls who worked for Dr. Amiel—that it wouldn't be long before he attracted the attention of movie producers. A man like that? Only in Hollywood!

And when his photograph came out in the newspapers, Teodora still couldn't believe her eyes.

"He favors Ucrós," said Argenis. "That same 'Life's a blast!' look, but more elegant."

"It isn't him," said Teodora. "And what if it is?"

Until her young Galaor came back home, nothing had any meaning for her. Not even the admiration showered on her by Dr. Manuel Amiel, a special, an extraordinary, man. A man she could love, were it not for that helpless boy she had sworn to protect.

Born in Real del Marqués, the son of a wealthy widower, Amiel had been brought up like a prince by his mother's sisters, the Laffaurie girls. Sent to study law and finance in Paris, he had fallen in love there with Ulla Ekland, a kitchen maid, and had given up the Sorbonne for a chef's hat. Madly taken with Ulla, he had married her and been a happy husband until they returned to his homeland, where his Nordic bride, reacting to the warmth of Caribbean shores, underwent a vertiginous transformation.

Blond blond, very *blond* blond. Hair so blond it was nearly white, and forget-me-not eyes. Ulla Amiel awakened a feverish admiration among the men of the coast. Men with kinky hair and dark skin; men with African features and clear blue eyes; men with sharp profiles and Indian eyelids; men with white skin, heavy eyebrows, and sensual lips; slender youths with broad shoulders. In short, she made the blood of both white and black boil; most of all, those with mixed blood, for whom the snowy lands of the north were as remote as the moon itself. Ulla, heady with power, thought of herself as a goddess of Valhalla, obliged to accept the adoration of her devoted.

She began to wear provocative dresses to parties at the Club Campestre, so everyone could admire the perfection of her body. She swam half naked in pools and at the beach. She did her shopping wearing see-through clothes and nothing underneath.

She posed as a forest sprite for a men's magazine, nude except for one orange leaf, and when the ladies of the tennis club found her honeysuckling with a black trainer and scandal erupted, she walked out on Dr. Amiel with Olympian calm.

She decided to live in Cartagena, because she adored the sun and the sea and the romantic nights. She rented a large house in the colonial section in harmony with her beauty. And every morning she appeared on the balcony, under the pretext of watering her hibiscus and *icaco* flowers, wrapped in a modestly closed silk bathrobe. She moved seductively, all sinuous blond hair, hips, legs, before the hungry and shameless stares of office workers, messenger boys, bank employees, produce sellers, itinerant vendors, fishermen, even respectable public figures. And when the area was crowded to bursting, she would suddenly untie the belt of her robe and shout one of her favorite Spanish phrases: "Thun-der-bolt!" revealing herself as she had come into the world.

At night she could be seen on Laguito beach or in the pool of the Hotel Caribe, escorted by young Cartagenans and sailors from the naval base, swimming not in salt or fresh water, but from one pair of arms to another, from one series of kisses to another.

This situation could not go on. It was too much indulgence for locals and tourists alike. At the request of the ladies, the tourist authority asked Ulla Amiel to leave the city; she was deported to Santa Marta, where she wore out her welcome in less than six months. From there she went to Curaçao, then to the Bahamas, then Hawaii, and finally she sank out of sight in Cannes, perhaps disheartened. For on the Côte d'Azur her charms maddened no one, since on any good day there were blondes to be plucked like bunches of grapes.

So Dr. Amiel inherited all Ulla's bikinis and photographs and became a free man. Free to love Teodora Vencejos and lead her to the altar, if she accepted.

As far as Teodora was concerned, however, the doctor's emotions did not make a dent in her own preoccupations: the absent Galaor Ucrós and her neighbor Clavel Quintanilla. Mysteriously, the handsome gallant of urban gossip and magenta convertible had been transformed into Galaor Ucrós. Not content with his models and singers and beauty queens, in the evenings he was also hotly courting Copelia Arantza, the eldest of the four sisters, without detouring to say hello to his mother's goddaughter, the woman with whom he had shared his childhood.

"Watch my car," he would tell the young kids in the plaza.

As for Clavel Quintanilla, she bore Galaor's rejection with aplomb. During the day she performed various tasks in the dry-goods store of Alí Sufyan, who had taken her on at Teodora's recommendation. Dusting shelves and counters, serving coffee, washing floors, and sweeping the brick sidewalk.

The money she made, she grumbled, barely covered rent

and milk for the baby. Asisclo Alandete continued to carry meals to her. How could you let a new mother starve? In the end, Teodora arranged to have Visitación Palomino look after Clavel's nutritional needs.

"The baby is Galaor's daughter, and she needs the care of a well-nourished mother."

Clavel also sent Teodora notes with repeated demands for money. One week she needed medicines, another diapers, and still another, money to have nighties made. To be on the safe side, she always wrote in the name of "the granddaughter of Ramona Ucrós," and although she said she didn't want to take advantage, neither did she hold back.

"It's her obligation," she boasted to Doña Argenis and Visitación Palomino (a.k.a. the Black Dove). "Teodora promised to look after Galaor, and my baby Esmaracola is his daughter. Besides, she's not even doing my laundry anymore!"

Teodora worked every day, even holidays. Despite her inheritance, she still was unable to buy a new dress or lipstick. She had no time, even in her dreams, to entice the runaway to her. Clavel, on the other hand, every Sunday evening, baby in arms, went down to stroll around the plaza where the Arantza sisters lived. All gussied up, switching her hips, sure of her power. The money she earned from the Turk Alí Sufyan (who in fact was Arab) was spent on witches, pythonesses, and women who read tobacco grains.

Every Friday she bought alum to dissolve in her famous sugarbush and then proudly proclaimed: "Every man likes to find his woman nice and tight, and that I am. Tight, tight, tight!"

She bathed in water scented with rosemary and maidenwort and lathered herself in *cariaquito morado* soap. For the house, she sprayed and burned incense every day, to drive off bad luck and attract love to her bed: Seven Spirits, Summoner, Triumph, Path-Clearer, Bronco-Breaker, Honeysuckle, Holy Night, Macaw Nest, Horn Divine, Husband-Binder. She had vowed to travel to Venezuela, to the sanctuary of María Lionza, the Goddess of Love, if the goddess got her man in line.

"Galaor will be back, oh, he'll be back! Or my name isn't Clavel! He's mine, all mine! No Copelia Arantza or Teodora Vencejos has what I have! They can't take him away from me." And she begged, "Help me, María Lionza!"

RAIN

Eldorado Airport was fogged in, and a whitish drizzle combed the Bogotá savannah. The Iberia jet circled the landing strip for ten minutes before being rerouted to Cali. Inclement winter weather reigned throughout the country, and air traffic was in chaos. Teodora, who had been unable to rid herself of Salustio Grimaldo in Puerto Rico, found herself, surprisingly, free. The coffee and sugarcane king, with all juices flowing, decided that the women of Cali were the most beautiful on the planet and (with his dynamic bodyguards) set off after a pair of spectacular twins poured into skin-tight shorts cut to reveal belly button and thighs.

It was another twelve hours before Teodora descended the steps of the plane in Soledad Airport—fatigued, hollow-eyed, her dress a mass of wrinkles. Thanks to the sweltering heat of the Atlantic coast.

"Whoooeeee! You one shake-and-bake mama, I'd like to eat you up to the last crumb!"

"Ay-ay-ay, mamita!"

All eyes focused on Teodora. Men admired her bare skin slicked with sweat, relished the acid tang of underarms and orifices. Women were wary, disdainful, with that self-assurance they reserve for beautiful rivals who are in difficult times, without a man at their side. A group of chattering gringo tourists openly laughed, at her expense.

Outside, rain was falling in torrents.

Teodora claimed her many suitcases, paid the skycap, and climbed into a rattletrap of a taxi, a Ford that had been discontinued in the fifties. Its driver was a mulatto with hair like cotton bolls and a wide grin that revealed missing teeth.

"I'd forgot how hot it is!"

Her silk blouse was transparent against her breasts. Sweat streamed down her hams and puddled her stomach. Her hair and underpants stuck to her like glue. Clearly, she could not present herself to Galaor and the girls in such a state. So she asked the taxi driver to take her to a quiet hotel—in Barranquilla—where she could rest, shower, and resuscitate the elegant woman who had set off from Madrid.

The driver explained that it had been raining for hours in Barranquilla and that the water raging through the streets would swamp his ancient automobile. He advised her that until things improved she should stop in Real del Marqués.

There weren't any real hotels there, but it had two acceptable boardinghouses. The one in the home of Doña Argenis, and El Hospedaje, owned by a black woman named Visitación Palomino.

"What?" Teodora was startled. "Isn't there a Hotel Ramona run by Don Galaor Ucrós?"

"Sheesss," he whistled. "You could call it that. But if I were you, I wouldn't stay there. You'll be better off with Doña Argenis. She keeps a clean place and a good kitchen."

"I'd forgot how hot it is," Teodora exclaimed a second time.

"But the air smells divine. Like *lulos* and tamarinds, green mangos and *guanábanas*. Ayyyyy! And a whiff of the drumstick tree. That's strange ... this morning it smelled like mud and shit."

Through glimmering threads of rain, Teodora caught a glimpse of the American Bar, and her heart began to thump uneasily. From a large locust tree, two soaked cats leapt onto the hood of the taxi and peered in at Teodora through the half-moons left by the windshield wipers. As the driver turned toward the heart of town, he nearly struck a burro staggering beneath the weight of two riders, one of them a large blond man, barefoot, too drunk to be aware of the danger.

"Hup, hooooo! Hey-up, burro!"

Only the two top buttons of his black-and-yellow checked shirt were buttoned; his soft, pink stomach spilled over the top of ragged pants like a flan too big for the cup. On the burro's haunches, as drunk as the man, her encircling arms clutching the man possessively, rode a girl in a bright print dress. The taxi driver allowed the fat man, tottering dangerously on his precarious perch, to cross. Teodora thought he looked vaguely familiar, the chubby cheeks, the red-gold mustache, the turned-up nose. Perhaps if she had seen his eyes, his name would have come to mind. But the drunk was wearing dark glasses and a white, obviously expensive sombrero pulled down to his eyebrows.

"Some guys are lucky," the driver commented as the man on the burro rode on down the street, one hand holding the reins and the other an uptilted bottle of white rum.

They had to drive around the block before finding a parking place near Calle de las Camelias, where Teodora's house, now a hotel, was located. The hearth where Ramonita Ucrós had brought her up on *yuca*, yams, white rice, black coffee, and the marrow of stew bones. The place where she had fallen madly in love with young Galaor. Without realizing it.

It had rained all week, and the road was covered with mud. The taxi driver, fearing for his obsolete conveyance, helped Teodora carry her luggage into the Residencias Argenis, located in the house where Clavel Quintanilla once had lived. Argenis Cervera's shop, in turn, was gone, and now a sign announced lodging in El Hospedaje, the establishment run by Visitación. A neon sign spelled out the name of the Hotel Ramona, and tiny blinking lights proclaimed a bar-cafeteria and an international menu, but everything was closed.

Darting lizards of sun rays played among the clouds. Cats yowled, mating in the middle of the day. Locust trees were burgeoning. A dark, handsome boy carried Teodora's suitcases for her. She recognized Perucho by the way he walked. Because of the downpour, no one had gone to work, and the residents, both boarding and transient, were all in the dining room, partaking, variously, of coffee, water, lemonade, and cold *avena*. Four traveling salesmen were playing cards at a table by the window. Two curly-headed fellows from Medellín in T-shirts, a man from the coast in a bright guayabera shirt, and a jean-clad man from Bogotá. At another table two cosmetics demonstrators were yawning uncontrollably, with unhappy faces. Beyond them, a secretary was painting her fingernails and confiding to another woman, a telephone-office employee, the story of her unhappy love affairs. All four women pretended not to hear the cacophony of the cats. It was a terrible season for hotel owners. Doña Argenis's best, newly constructed rooms with private baths and large windows overlooking the street stood empty. She barely glanced at Teodora's passport. And did not recognize her at all.

Suddenly, there were gurglings and cooings from the doves in the eaves. The rain began to slacken. Doña Argenis, her nerves rubbed raw by the cats' matings, ran to check on her lovebirds.

"That's odd," she murmured.

"What's odd?" Perucho's voice was high as a woman's.

"They were so downcast I thought they had the pip. And now they're doing the same thing the cats are. Making out like lovebirds!"

"What?"

"You have to see it to believe it."

The hotel across the street, without a sign of life in the middle of the morning, worried Teodora. Was it because of the rain? It was no longer coming down by the bucketful, but the street was still like a river and impossible to cross. The taxi driver, who had gone out to put his car in a safe place, came back looking like a drowned rooster and bearing amazing news. The almond trees on the Plaza Mayor, which the day before had been dying, had new leaves and were putting out buds and flowers. Everyone went outside to sing and splash in the water.

One of the salesmen tuned in Radio Melodía. An oily voice was singing, with great feeling,

> A sudden burst of flame
> turned our lives to cinders,
> leaving only ash
> where love once hotly glowed.

The man in the guayabera asked the telephone operator to dance, and one of the curly-headed customers ordered a shot and a beer chaser. Don Rufino Cervera, who had been beating his brains out at a corner table over numbers, pesos, and bills, had an inspiration. He ran to the kitchen to fry up small meat pies, corn griddlecakes, and tiny sausages. As he went by, he massaged his wife's impressive nether regions. He craved action! *Viva la rumba!* he cried, as he tossed down the first shot of rum.

On an impulse, Teodora paid for a week in advance without identifying herself. Doña Argenis Cervera, impressed by the bearing and elegance of the traveler, offered to bring a cool drink to her room. No. No, thank you. Teodora did not want to be burdened with unvoiced questions and said she would prefer a bowl of broth. She savored it in the dining room, in the company of the taxi driver, while the other guests danced cheek to cheek, rubbing against each other's legs. Salesmen and working girls were glowing with happiness, as if they had just taken notice of their bodies and desires.

Not revealing her identity to Doña Argenis was another of Teodora's irresistible whims. A foolish fancy, just like her inopportune trip. Could they have been flashes of intuition? What a shame, she told herself, that Dr. Amiel wasn't there. He would know how to set things in order.

"I feel restless," she muttered when she went to her room. Traces of cinnamon and musk essences lingered on her sweaty skin. The heat and the sound of the music added to the caterwauling on the rooftops exhausted her before she could bathe. And she collapsed onto a lightly starched sheet that smelled of lemon and verbena. The cool scents of her life.

With trembling heart and with the image of Galaor Ucrós struggling to withstand the malicious smile of Dr. Amiel, Teodora Vencejos fell asleep.

RUFFLES AND ORANGE BLOSSOMS

One day Clavel Quintanilla loaded her furniture into a van and with her daughter in her arms moved to the neighborhood where the Arantza sisters lived. Her house was near the plaza; it had two floors, balconies, large windows. From every angle she could keep a close watch on Galaor Ucrós and insult him with ear-splitting screams when he drove up in a new crimson automobile to pay court to the oldest Arantza, Copelia. Visits carried out, in the mode of warm climates, with open doors.

Clavel often sent her little girl, baptized Esmaracola and now barely two years old, dressed in clothes threadbare from washing and with toes poking out of her shoes, carrying succinct notes that read, "I need shoes," "I want a dolly," "Milk!," "Bread." The same requests that softened up Teodora, whom

Clavel hounded for money with the tenacity of a rabid flea, had no success with Galaor. The romance remained intact.

Copelia Arantza, head over heels in love, and at the counsel of her family, held firm before Clavel's frenzied parading up one street and down another, her insults, her pleas for pity through Esmaracola, even her threats of suicide.

"Don't give an inch," Copelia's mother said. "Galaor is your formal suitor. Do not let that wicked woman take him from you."

Meanwhile, Teodora, with her unvoiced and hopeless love, was working all day and part of the night. The income from her inheritance evaporated as soon as it was received, thanks to taxes on the farms, the workers' back pay, and countless debts run up first by Doña Ramonita Ucrós and then by Galaor, in her name. Besides that, she kept lending money to neighbors in need, and was helping Padre Imeldo Villamarín repair the rundown church of Real del Marqués. The faithful were many, but they had no money and were not given to marrying. They baptized and confirmed their children and celebrated First Communions, but most paid with a hen, a basket of yams or *yuca*, bananas or tamarinds. And the parish church needed immediate attention. The cupola was crumbling, and red ants and termites were destroying the doors, windows, and confessionals. Bedbugs streamed from the saints' eyes like tears. At times there was not enough money for candles on the main altar.

Teodora was also paying for incense. She had hopes of

moving the Virgen del Milagro and San Antonio, her blessed patron saints. Sunday after Sunday she pleaded, "Bring Galaor back to my care!" because how else could she fulfill the promise she had made to her madrina? If it was best, let him marry the eldest of the Arantza girls, raise children, and take his place as an honorable man. Was that too much to ask?

Everyone in Real del Marqués and Barranquilla—even, apparently, in Malambo, Usiacurí, and Soledad—was already talking about the marriage. Copelia Arantza, who for seven years had worked as executive secretary in the Banco del Atlántico, gave credence to the rumors when she resigned her position. She was assembling a trousseau. She had picked out a house and furniture. She wrote and rewrote guest lists.

"I wonder just how long Galaor Ucrós's luck can last," commented Dr. Amiel, who was in charge of the wedding cake. A fantasy with nine layers, pink hearts and flowers, and the classic bride and groom on top.

"What do you mean, Doctor?" Teodora asked.

"Galaor Ucrós has less feeling than a post or a pillar of salt. He's nothing more than a good-looking stud. The only thing he knows for sure how to do is screw."

"Doctor, don't talk like that! Don Galaor is talented. He knows how to play the piano and the violin."

"I hope he hurries up and gets married and is happy," Amiel continued serenely. "He doesn't deserve it, but that would get him off your back."

"Not another word," Teodora said stiffly.

The doctor's wishes did not, however, bring about the desired nuptials. That much dreamed-of wedding capsized under the weight of bad luck. Concerned about Copelia's interests, as any devoted suitor would be, Galaor accompanied her to collect the pension for her seven years' employment in the bank. Then, since she had to go to a shower, she asked Galaor to deposit the juicy check in her personal account in a different bank. He had a date that night to meet Señora Arantza and Copelia's younger sisters in the Hotel del Prado, where a group of former students of the École Française were entertaining his betrothed.

Galaor Ucrós, poor man, never reached the Hotel del Prado. He was assaulted by footpads while crossing a street. The check was stolen from him and cashed the same day, and he was beaten within an inch of his life. Pulled from the sea at Bocas de Ceniza by men in a small boat, he was nursed back to health by charitable souls. When, after many days, he returned to the land of the living, he was too dazed to remember what had happened. The address, house, street, as well as the names of his benefactors had vanished from his mind.

"What do you bet that those 'benefactors' were the famous nieces of La Payares? Poor old Ucrós. So defenseless." Dr. Amiel's irony was thick. "The way I heard it, there was a spree that lasted two weeks. Many a white wine cork was pulled, and whisky, Del Valle, and white rum flowed like water. Pigs and hens were killed, and coconut rice, posta negra, and a *fritanga* were served every day. The host spent his days in his underwear, playing poker and dice, bedding Leocadia and her purported nieces by turn, and just in general horsing around. They say he played a violin solo buck naked."

"How can you repeat such lies, Doctor!" Teodora protested.

"They took pictures, because there was also an exhibition of totem poles, with Galaor both in and out of the running."

"I don't hear this. I'm not listening."

In the market in Barranquilla and Real del Marqués, in the bars and houses of ill repute in Barrio Abajo and Rebolo, an album documenting a memorable contest was for sale. There were photos for all tastes and appetites, and to every sailing mast clung a stark-naked girl with eager hands: face covered, legs spread, breasts in full flower—all in living color! On view were rosy little peckers, like cherubim, beneath enormous beer bellies; pencil penises with worn-down erasers set on athletic bodies; unprepossessing but triumphant, pricks like glazed sweetmeats; cockadoodledoos with dangling wattles; heliotrope dongs and plummy testicles, along with an assortment of earthworms and nightcrawlers. There were loaves of French bread and hard rolls and piccolos and boomerangs, and balls like fritters, and pale ones and veiny ones and balls of universal cut. But the family jewels of Galaor Ucrós ... uhmmmm-uhmmmm. A sawed-off shotgun, primed for action, wreathed with brilliant red-and-gold hair. Out of this world! Which was, after all, why he was called Golden Rod. He had the reputation of being a die-hard dick who could spark fire from any tinder.

How could anyone be so barbaric as to show that trash to Teodora? Even though the album was a success in under-the-counter sales, Dr. Manuel Amiel did not have the heart to use it. It could destroy his rival, but it might also turn Teodora against him. In anger and spite, he ordered his assistants to bake a wedding cake identical to the one Copelia Arantza had ordered and positioned atop it a naked couple sitting astride a pearly seesaw. Meanwhile, the wedding cake itself arrived in good hour at the Club Campestre, where the reception was to be held. A work of culinary art, which by irony of fate was later sold back to Amiel at half price and exhibited in the shop window of his ice cream parlor-cum-cafe, attracting many customers.

Both cakes served to initiate a promising career as specialist in baked goods and aphrodisiacs. Amiel's customers, friends, and suppliers, using one pretext or other, began to request "different" and novel cakes, and sweet and savory hors d'oeuvres, for private parties and romantic rendezvous.

Dr. Amiel had not tried to silence his assistants.

The wedding of Galaor Ucrós and Copelia Arantza, reported by *El Heraldo*, the *Diario del Caribe*, *El Tiempo*, *El Espectador*, and *El Siglo*, which was to be celebrated amid arches, lilies, and orange blossoms, ended in a tragedy worthy of the Milan opera. When the bride, floating in a mist of lace and tulle, and escorted by her younger sisters, Aída and Semírisis, arrived at the atrium of the church, she was bushwacked by La Quintanilla.

"Husband-snatcherrrr!" Clavel screamed as she tore off the bride's veil and coronet and transformed an elegant coiffure into a hen's nest.

"I'll just run along and get the authorities," Galaor said to his friends, and abandoned the church under full steam.

Terrified attendants and guests were unable to react quickly enough. Clavel Quintanilla, in black down to her toes, pummeled and bit and kicked La Arantza, leaving her bedraggled as a beggar. At one point, they did manage to subdue Clavel, yes, but neglected to cover her mouth. And how she howled!

"I am six months pregnant, and the father of my child is Galaor Ucrós. I want the world to know! Serpent! Bag of bones! Jezebel! My new double bed was bought with your money, you featherbrain! You want to know where your money went? Ask Leocadia Payares and her girls!"

The name Leocadia Payares was too much for Copelia, who already had her suspicions about the matter because of the giggles and whispers and elbowing that followed them when she went for a stroll on Galaor's arm. She couldn't forget how the gamblers and idlers came out of the American Bar, interrupting their dice and billiards, to stare at her. And the story about the album had been heard in the bank.

Her love died that day. No. No! She would not live the rest of her life putting up with Galaor's bastard children or the insults of his kept woman. She stopped the first taxi she saw and withdrew, orange blossoms, ruffles, and tulle in tatters. Makeup tear-streaked and bruises darkening. At last liberated from the love that had consumed her for years. Which she quickly demonstrated by marrying a bank manager who had courted her fervently but without hope.

When Galaor returned to the church a half hour later with an officer and two policemen, he found the church empty. Even Padre Imeldo Villamarín had deserted.

CHICKS

. . . In Cati's bed

> *I was a'lyin',*
> *she in her bed*
> *and I in hers.*
> *She was a'cryin'. . .*

crooned a male voice as Teodora awakened to a dawn
drenched in a sun multiplied in dancing sequins. Outside,
birds were billing and cooing in the rain-wet branches of
almond and locust trees. Water was singing through the
canals. Teodora opened the window and breathed fresh air
fragrant with wet earth, leaves, and resins. Turquoise blue
waves flowed from the horizon. In the frame of the window
were newly woven nests with lavender eggs. The lickerish
voice was licking each word:

. . . She was a'cryin'
cause she was a maiden,
and I was a'crying
as I made her mine.

Teodora predicted a perfect day as she lingered in the shower.

In the guests' dining room she was greeted with complicitous, paired smiles. Traveling men and telephone operators, nurses and clerks. Hand in hand, eyes sparkling, legs touching. Little treats passed back and forth across the tablecloth.

"Whose little lips are smeared with eggs now?"

Teodora, in a simple white cotton dress and comfortable sandals, was surprised to see the taxi driver, who handed her a bouquet of roses.

"They bloomed last night, and from a bare stalk," he explained. "And they smell just like you. I'm at your service. My name is Durango Berrío."

"Strange," said Doña Argenis, who was serving coffee. "You smell just like a friend of mine. I dreamed about her last night."

"So where are we off to today, señá?" the taxi driver asked as Teodora finished her breakfast.

The streets were a quagmire, and it took them half an hour to reach the telephone office on the plaza. Nor was it much easier to get through to Madrid. Toñi, the doctor's housekeeper, was weeping when she answered the telephone. Amiel had canceled his trip to Berlin and was locked in his office. Not eating or drinking.

"What's the matter with him? Is he crazy?"

"He won't eat a bite until you come back."

"I have a right to visit my husband!"

"He wants to kill himself."

"Tell him, from me, to go ahead!"

Teodora slammed down the phone, disgusted. Amiel was a dyed-in-the-wool dictator and was treating her like a slave. It was time to declare her independence. She had to do it. But would Galaor recognize her? She must not doubt ... After all, weren't they a single being, a one and only love, one soul? When she passed Alí Sufyan's dry-goods store, she walked a little faster and did not glance inside. Both the Turk (actually an Arab) and his wife, Zulema, had a merchant's sharp eye and could set off alarm bells. And discovering Teodora, his Teodora, beneath the elegant woman, was a surprise to be reserved for Don Galaor.

The streets were swarming. Fierce clouds rolled across the skies, and the rising wind foretold rain. Durango, cautious, did not dare turn his rattletrap into the Calle de las Camelias—a kind of channel between raised sidewalks—in case the rain let loose with force. Gallant, however, he accompanied Teodora back to the Residencias Argenis.

"What do I owe you?"

"Nothing, s'rita."

"I insist. You can't work for nothing."

"Well, then, buy me a lottery ticket. I dreamed last night of eights and sevens. I need a new taxi, and I owe money to young Perucho."

They walked along the sidewalk until they found a ticket seller, and instead of eighty-seven, Teodora decided on seventy-eight. Durango asked only for a partial ticket, but Teodora bought the whole thing.

"With two conditions. First, one half of the ticket is for Perucho, and second, now I want you to go with me to the Hotel Ramona."

"Why do you want to go there, señá? You're better off where you are."

They crossed the street on boards laid to keep pedestrians from sinking into the mud, just as a tall woman with huge hips, arms and legs like pillows, and a face round as the moon was entering the hotel. Six children between eleven and three walked on either side. Two clutching her hands and the others her skirts.

"Morning, Doña," said Durango.

"Morning," the woman replied disdainfully.

The face was familiar to Teodora. She had seen the triumphant gleam of those eyes, the smug, satisfied face, the overweening pride. But she didn't dare ask who she was. She didn't want to alert the driver to her own identity.

"Some women have all the luck," Durango remarked. "Even when they don't deserve it."

On the terrace a skinny servant girl was sweeping away the leaves and mud left by the cloudburst. Then Teodora saw her daughter Esmaracola. Barefoot, in a cotton blouse too tight around her breasts and brief shorts that revealed sturdy thighs. She had grown so much in three years! Or was it four? She was swinging in a hammock strung between two columns, reading a cheap romance and nonchalantly eating *mamoncillos* and tossing the seeds and skins onto the tiles imported from Italy, into the street, in the direction of the broom.

"That takes the cake!" exclaimed Durango. "Listen, Mara! Don't be a pig. That's how the drains get stopped up."

"Mind your own business, fatass" was Esmaracola's retort as she shied a half-eaten *mamoncillo* at him, which he skillfully dodged.

"Sorry, señá." Durango glanced toward Teodora with embarrassment. "This is no place for you. Let's come back another day."

"What is going on here? Is this a hotel, or isn't it?" she asked.

"Hotel? Ha! That's one way to put it."

"I don't understand."

Durango Berrío smiled maliciously, showing missing teeth and one gold crown.

"The Hotel Ramona is a hotel when Galaor Ucrós's legitimate wife shows up. She's living across the pond, over there in Spain. I've never met her. I've only been here two years."

"I still don't understand."

"By calling it a hotel, Don Galaor gets money out of his wife. That's the long and short of it! Now, we'd better go, doñita. It's time for lunch, and there's nothing worth eating here."

"I want to see everything. We'll have lunch here."

The vestibule was strewn with mango peels, chewing-gum wrappers, and soaking-wet magazines. Demetria was behind the reception desk, watching television. When Durango asked whether the dining room was open, her eyes never left the noontime soap opera.

"If Mama feels like it, I guess it is. Although I doubt it."

Lined up against the wall and large windows looking out over the garden and terrace were tables with checked cloths, water glasses, and vases with plastic carnations (*claveles* for the lovely Clavel!). A thin layer of dust lay over everything. Dried locust blossoms and thick cobwebs hung in the corners. At the largest table, which had no cloth, the children Teodora had seen with the tall, large-hipped, moon-faced woman were eating lunch. Plunging fingers into the stew, ripping hunks of meat from the ribs, throwing pieces of *yuca* and plantains. They laughed and jostled and made faces at Teodora. The youngest boy stood up on his chair, dropped his pants, and began to sing in a small but mellifluous voice, "Little chickies say 'pee-pee, pee-pee.'" A mound of sheets and dirty clothes piled on two benches exuded a strong odor of urine. But even stronger fumes emanated from deeper inside the hotel, from the direction where Ramonita Ucrós (née De Céspedes) had had her bathroom, her closet and dressing room, and a room for sewing, writing bills, and listening to music.

No one came to help them or ask what they wanted for lunch. Through the open windows, in the overgrown garden, Teodora saw the Spanish fountain she had bought in Seville and shipped by sea now being used for laundry. In the middle of the grass and weeds choking out the roses and jasmine, among the empty bottles and broken crates beneath the plum trees Teodora had never allowed to be cut down, an old man in a canvas chair sat eating. Barefoot, legs sprawled, he was snagging sardines from an enormous tin. Grease was running out the corners of his mouth and dripping from his mustache, but he wiped it away with chunks of bread he then wolfed down greedily. In his eyes shone the memory of many, many hungry days and the full satisfaction of savoring his favorite food. Teodora felt, alternately, embarrassment and happiness for him.

"This is the life!" he exclaimed, winking a cunning eye as he toasted her—"Glug, glug"—with a beer.

"That's Don Galaor's father-in-law. He worked all his life as a porter in the market in Barranquilla. Now he's taking it easy, stuffing himself to the gills."

And as Teodora's face had turned white with disbelief, Durango Berrío explained.

"The father of the other woman, Don Galaor's lover.

They have seven kids and have a rip-roaring fight every month. Since he has such an appetite for the women."

"He has other women?"

"A formal sweetheart who lives on the plaza, the youngest of the Del Rosal sisters. Another woman with three kids down by the port. And now he's trying out something new." The taxi driver grew expansive. "A real doozie! A little chick who gets drunk with him and goes along on his sprees."

Teodora did not listen to the details. A bright light was dawning in her brain, as if someone had applied a magic ointment to cure her of blindness.

"Where is Don Galaor now?"

"Who knows? Here, or where his other woman lives, snoring away his siesta somewhere. Listen, it's getting hot and my stomach's growling. Can't we go?"

"There's something else I want to do," she said.

As they left the dining room, the clamor of the kids did not skip a beat nor did the old man outside interrupt his gluttonous feast. Things were winding down in the kitchen, where a young girl was scrubbing the enormous pot the rice had been cooked in. She did not even turn to look at them.

Most of the rooms on the second floor, ten facing the patio and ten overlooking the street, were closed off. The barnyard smell was coming from the rear, from the music and TV room, a place Teodora had dreamed down to the last millimeter, with its easy chairs, assorted magazines, and bar stocked with the best liquors. Along with the nauseating smell, the decibel level and clacking were growing steadily stronger.

"What is that noise, anyway?"

Durango Berrío limited himself to throwing a miserable glance at Teodora.

In the corridor was a small woman in a bottle-green dress and red hair from a bottle; her right foot was in a basin of soapy water and the other was propped on a chair. A manicurist was painting her clawlike toenails with a solferino-hued polish.

"Come, come! Come on in!" she invited. "I have the best hens on all the coast. Why, they come from Barranquilla and Cartagena to buy them. And there are fresh eggs if you want them."

The music and TV room did not live up to its name. In the place of furniture, television set, and sound equipment, Teodora saw nothing but hens. Coops and feed trays rose to the ceiling. The floor was covered with straw. Chicks were fluttering from one side to another, and eggs gathered that day were piled in a large basket.

"Pure nourishment," the woman said. "How many do you want, Durango?"

"Four dozen," said Teodora, as if she wanted to separate yolk and whites from gall.

"I'll send them to you tonight. After they've prettied me

up."

"A fine henhouse you have here."

"Thanks to my daughter Clavito. Since she doesn't give a fig for running a hotel, she lets me have my own business. She's a good daughter."

Suddenly, blood-curdling screams shattered the afternoon stillness. Between gasps came a woman's voice. "Helllllup, ay-ay-ay, I can't take any moooore! Do it now-ow-ow! Like thaaaaaaat." With ay-ays and ye-es-eses that would curl the hair even of someone who'd heard everything.

Drawn by those ay-ays, Teodora, clinging to the peeling railing in the corridor, ran toward the back of the house where Ramonita Ucrós (née De Céspedes) once had her bedroom, her sitting room for intimate visits, and her altar for San Judas Tadeo and Santa Rose de Lima. "Ayyy, I'm dyyying. Now! Now! I want it now-ow-ow-ow!"

The bedroom was in shadow, the shutters closed over burlap-covered windows. The large bed still dominated the room. There beneath the mosquito netting was the fat man Teodora had seen teetering atop the burro and swigging white rum, rippling buttocks and belly pumping like a bellows between the legs of the woman with the pillowy arms. He stark naked and she with her skirt up to her neck, both of them huffing and puffing like seals on the bright red sheets. From beneath his soft, doughy breadbasket, divided into several loaves, rose a rooster with a half-wrung neck. Galaor's hand was deep-sea diving into the shadows of

Clavel's inky sea urchin, as she moaned and herself groped below enormous spheres, one of which displayed a belly button protruding like a second shrunken cock.

"Galaor?" Teodora whispered, incredulous. "And she? Who is she?"

"Clavel Quintanilla, his paramour."

Teodora stood in a daze, contemplating the man of her dreams, her handsome Galaor, the inheritance bequeathed her on Doña Ramonita Ucrós's deathbed. Her white knight? Was this a joke? This was a freshly butchered hog, scalded and scraped and cured with bicarbonate of soda and saffron. A worthless body, as Dr. Amiel had said. Teodora fled the room, shaken by an unexpected gale of laughter that burned deep in her being, rose from her solar plexus, and singed her palate. No! No-o-o! That mountain of flab could not be her handsome Galaor Ucrós. Impossible! That ... that ... that *that*! That tub of butter and guts! No! Someone was lying! Either this wasn't real, or the laughter threatening to wrench her bones from her joints was affecting her sanity.

"Señá, señaaaa!" cried Durango Berrío. "What is it, s'rita?"

The laughter was warm, treacherous, rib-tickling, and it spread to Teodora's thighs and the shell of her ears. It crawled up her hips, blazed on her pubis, pierced the throat of her ringdove like an arrow. She laughed and laughed, wildly, as she tore off her blouse, her skirt, her fine cotton undergarments, her sandals. Even her skin was too much!

She tossed her belongings into the air, into the face of Durango Berrío, who ran after her through the rooms and down the stairs of the hotel toward the exit.

"Help her, Don Perucho."

In vain, Perucho Cervera, mobilized by the outcry, ran out the door of the Residencias Argenis to intercept Teodora. She, gamboling in the buff, pirouetted across the planks linking the two sidewalks, splendid in her laughter and her nudity, shouting to the four winds: "Golden Rod? No! Galaor Ucrós does not have a rod of gold. Not . . . any . . . longer!" And lightly, gracefully, her thirty-pounds-slimmer body fell into the marbled gray and terra-cotta mud oozing down the Calle de las Camelias.

MEPHISTO

Teodora did not receive an invitation to the wedding of Copelia Arantza and Galaor, but in the market she heard about the horrifying dénouement and wept oceans for her beloved's bad fortune. No. She could not understand, not even imagine, the twisted sentiments of a woman capable of ridiculing a man as handsome, intelligent, and sensitive as the son of Ramonita Ucrós.

And what people were saying! That the sweethearts had sneaked a taste of the cake early and gone to little hotels along the coast highway, and that Copelia had not been convinced by the highly touted golden flute Ucrós took so much pride in. Where was its music? Its vaunted symphonic power? she had asked herself. La Quintanilla had played such a demanding tune on that instrument that it was about played out. And she, Copelia, did not want a tin whistle in her bed.

"Have you heard the news, S'ita Teodora?" the fishermen would ask sympathetically as they cleaned their *barbules* and *bocachicas* and *mojarras*.

"No, I don't know anything."

"Someone needs to strike a match to that man of yours, s'ita. If he's gonna keep you *and* that carnation lady happy. What can I give you today?"

"I don't want anything."

"Nothing! But it's your turn, doñita," the women selling ceviche and oysters would say as they insolently patted their hips. "If you don't hurry, they're going to steal a husband away from you. Look, you have to give a man a snack now and then, a little butter and salt. You have a toasty oven, don't you? So get going! Some women go after a man like a piranha. They suck him dry, whoosh!, like a mussel. And if you don't put up a fight . . . "

Teodora would march away without finishing her shopping. She was horrified, because beneath her compassion she was beginning to feel an uncontainable joy. Her secret love was thawing, and her desires (never expressed, never dreamed) had her little clam like mamey pulp rubbed with hot chili and red pepper.

To try to quench the fire, Teodora bathed three and four times a day. She did not go to the police to declare the theft of her jewels, which had vanished as if by magic. She did not want to incriminate Galaor, the one person—except for Padre Imeldo—who knew about the hiding place under the floor tiles. And if he had not been the one who took them, then who? They belonged to Doña Ramonita, and a man with wounded pride can do foolish things, like steal, or kill himself, or throw himself into gambling or rum. He was too innocent to consider cocaine or other drugs. Nevertheless, she feared for his reason.

One night when she returned home, she found Galaor's suitcases—with the raised initials—his golf clubs, his tennis rackets, his new upright piano, and his violin. It was obvious that he intended to take up residence again in Real del Marqués. So sensitive, Teodora grieved. The ridicule and insults he suffered before his friends over his failed marriage had been too much for him. Filled with pain, he had run to take refuge in the home of his ancestors, beside the sister of his heart.

She didn't see him. No. It was like living with an invisible man. Three, four weeks, hearing the street door and door to his bedroom close at dawn. Enough to savor, alone, lying on her narrow bed, an embarrassment of happiness. To feel she was, alternately, levitating and disappearing, like a floating star or rose petal blown by the wind. She didn't see him. No. She found his shirts, changed his bed, perfumed the air of the house to demonstrate her affection. Without so much as a note from Galaor. Shamed, saddened, he refused to face her. And she? Unable to console him, take him his coffee, have his dinner waiting, as she had in the days of Doña Ramonita. So sad! But she had to work. Early every morning she caught a bus to Barranquilla; many executives and secretaries ate breakfast in Dr. Amiel's cafés, and she supervised the preparation of the bread, muffins, fruit nectars, and cold salads, elbow to elbow with her boss.

Absorbed in her humble, quiet happiness, she did not know that people had begun to whisper, to slander, to drag her most noble sentiments through the dusty summer heat of her street, her neighborhood, the established—since colonial times—limits of the town named Real del Marqués.

"If I were you, I would throw that bum out in the street," Dr. Amiel said one morning.

"Who?" she asked crisply.

"Who do you think? That worthless body, Ucrós. He's living at your expense. He's pawned the jewels you inherited from your mother. Now he's making out he's a victim, whimpering and whining in bars, and singing I've-been-done-wrong songs. Showboat!"

"What are you trying to tell me, Doctor? I demand respect."

"Respect? Your reputation is getting ground into the dirt. Although I like you just the way you are. It isn't your fault. You were born naive. But other people don't think the same way."

"That's enough. Not another word. If my reputation is a little shaky, it's because of those naked women we bake for godless, lawless men."

Dr. Amiel sighed, ashamed of his outbursts, his jealousy,

his love. It was true that he was acquiring a terrible reputation because of the friends who asked him for titillating cakes. Brazen Venuses, plumped-hipped fairies, gigantic sugarbushes, tits encircled with diamonds. And cocks of various natures.

"I'm a businessman. I can't say no to good customers."

"Better to say nothing."

"All right, I'll say nothing." And with a rebellious slash, he exaggerated the line of the female sex on the cake he was decorating so meticulously.

It was a prophetic gesture. Soon his name would appear in major newspapers and would leap from the scandal sheets to show-biz and romance magazines. Even to books about cooking and glamour.

"I am going home," said Teodora, who did not officially have a set schedule. "No one can force me to work for a degenerate. If you do not stop doing big honey pots, I quit, Doctor."

"And that's how it is?"

"Yes."

The doctor had the devil by the tail. He cordially despised Ucrós, and decided, at whatever price, to save Teodora from him. More bills arrived every day: suits, shoes, sports equipment, IOUs from shops and even stalls in the market. Galaor Ucrós could not get enough! And Teodora, stupid girl she was, could only say: "It's all right, Doctor. I'll pay. It's my obligation. Please, just take it out of my salary."

Which he did. He withheld twenty or thirty thousand pesos a month, and the rest kept piling up.

"So you're quitting, eh?"

"That's what I said."

"Fine, as you wish. But first, tell your precious Galaor to pay me what he owes me. If not, I'll—"

Teodora looked at him, purple with rage.

"He will pay you every last centavo! That's the last straw." And, defiantly, "And the jewels belonged to my madrina, Ramonita Ucrós!"

That was when Dr. Amiel blew his top. In less than a month he destroyed a reputation as a baker and owner of the finest cafés and ice cream parlors on the Atlantic shore. He closed his establishments, lock, stock, and barrel, but exhibited bizarre merchandise in the attractively decorated windows. Not muffins or mille-feuilles or jelly rolls but a series of sculpted posteriors, sealed and parted, orifices clearly delineated, and even a few with real pipes and tobacco as stage dressing, with a single sign that announced to the world: LIFE IS FOR ASSHOLES.

And there was worse to come! Enormous cakes began to be delivered at weddings decorated with feverishly humping grooms and arrogant cocks and garlands formed of birth control pills, vulvas, even actual condoms; rosy breasts replaced sugar roses, the tits surrounded by candied fruit. Amiel even went so far as to scatter about little butterflies that instead of antennas displayed peewee peters with infinitesimal testicles. And mouths and tongues licking what . . .

"Our good doctor has gone too far," they say the mayor's wife said.

"The man's hot as a tick," commented her best friend, who had fewer inhibitions.

Both women attended a meeting of a group called We Love Our City, a committee whose members were important society ladies, nuns, housewives, professional women, and one or two avant-garde intellectuals. And, inflamed with patriotism, they agreed to march down the main streets of the city carrying placards and signs alluding to the corruptor of chaste girls and properly brought-up young men, to the evil bakery king capable of perverting elements as innocent as flour, milk, butter, and eggs. To the Mephisto who was forcing one truth down everyone's throat: that when all is said and done, people in love do not marry to please society but to bang their brains out behind closed doors. With nothing to stop them!

News of the ladies' project filtered out within minutes and galvanized the admirers and defenders of Dr. Amiel, who until that moment had kept out of sight. A very large crowd invaded the streets on the day of the protest, with orchestras and brass bands, creating a sort of improvised carnival. All the fancy women and females of dubious lineage came brandishing colorful panties and bikinis and bras on poles. They came on foot and on floats, and with commendable alacrity they had recruited gay queens and ladies of the far sidewalk and princesses of motels and rented rooms and spectacles of transvestites and nudists. They danced the samba, the mapalé, the lambada, dances that featured prow and stern. The crowd, besides rendering tribute to King Momo, bore aloft a happy couple (constructed of papier-mâché and flour and watercolor): Emperor Priapus and Queen Sugarbush on the verge of delirious fusion.

When the two parades met in the middle of Paseo Colón, ladies, fancy women, whores, nuns, exhibitionists, birds of many a feather, a monumental battle ensued, without interrupting the flow of rum, whisky, gin, or concentric ripples of fannyfeelies—which led to fascinating complications. The mayor's wife and her friend Bedelia were intoxicated by the mere fumes in the air and were seen wiggling their backsides in time with the music, breasts bared to the world. The mayor had to ask for police intervention.

All the women, every last one, believed that the uniformed men were sticking their nose in where they weren't needed, and set upon them with high heels, shoves, kisses, nibbles, and swipes of the tongue, targeting faces, bellies, knees, and rears indiscriminately. Even the Madre Consolata of the Daughters of God, along with Doña Digna Grueso, wife of the governor, and Doña Angeles Natera, wife of the mayor, became embroiled in the scuffle. All three ended up in the municipal jail, mixed in with girls who lived in houses with names like "Eyefuls" "Peter Piper's Pickled Pecker," "Bubblegum," "Juanita Banana," and others of that ilk. Not even Doña Bedelia Afanador, the best friend of the mayor's wife, escaped. Oh, no. Lost among the throng, she ended up in the arms of the owner of the Suavecito Bar, engaged first in mutual pawing, followed by an old-fashioned frigging fest. She gave up her children, her position, and her Blue Book ancestry to run off and live with him. What a life!

That, then, is the story of how Dr. Manuel Amiel came to be run out of town for having been the seed of the hurricane. A governmental edict forbade him to live in that province for a period of five years: for having been found guilty of offenses against morality, for having contributed to a public disturbance, and for having attempted to corrupt both local and national womanhood.

As he was preparing for his march into the desert, the adjudged, who had not attended the protest, decided to collect Teodora Vencejos's IOUs, everything she owed him.

TO DIE OF LOVE

Lying between damp sheets on an inflatable mattress on an iron bed, Teodora Vencejos opened her eyes and smiled into the void. Beside her sat the wife of Alí Sufyan, Zulema, cooling Teodora's brow with a towel dampened in ice water.

"Wake up, please," she begged.

Heat flowed from the curves and orifices of Teodora's naked body, swirled around the room, boiled beneath the floor, flooded through open windows, and hovered, invisible, in the acacias and *matarratones* surrounded by the magical mud that filled the Calle de las Camelias, now the center of a tourist attraction.

Zulema Sufyan's throat was dry. Sweat slicked the palms of her hands, ran down her back and thighs, soaked her fine cotton dress. Had it been up to her, she would have been as naked as Teodora Vencejos, but Alí was too jealous, he would never permit it!

"Wake up," she pleaded once more.

Teodora, as on other days, as she had for an entire year, from the moment she had fallen into her deep sopor, looked at Zulema for an instant, without recognizing her. Then she sat up with the slow movements of the blind, and her eyes came to rest on two blue lizards rubbing their bellies against the windowsill, perhaps looking at her, perhaps smelling her smell, completely enraptured.

"Lovely," she murmured to herself.

She drifted toward the window, unfastened the latch that held the sash, and rolled up the canvas cloth. The lizards dashed up her left arm, frolicked around her neck and shoulders, making joyful whistling noises, curled their tails, returned to the sill, and coupled in a delirious blue iridescence, as if Teodora's eyes had exercised some lunar influence over them.

"When will you truly wake up?" Zulema murmured.

The afternoon breeze carried off the pair of lizards. At twilight Teodora's fever waned, and the tourists bathing in the medicinal water and mud of the improvised baths began to retire. Doña Argenis Cervera came in, carrying clean sheets in her arms. Behind her, Visitación Palomino pushed a small cart with the only food Teodora's stomach would tolerate, strange coincidence, the concentrated broth of dove that in Doña Ramonita Ucrós's house had been reserved for

Galaor. Exactly what had been prescribed by the physician, Nemesio Donado, who had answered the Cervera family's hurried call one year earlier when, after they had pulled a beautiful stranger from the mud and administered artificial respiration, Perucho had thought he recognized Teodora.

"In fact it is Teodora," concurred Dr. Donado, who had attended her birth and treated her mumps and sporadic colds.

"What's the matter with her?" a chorus of three Cerveras inquired: Perucho, Doña Argenis, and Don Rufino.

"Several problems," he said. "She has a temperature, and her amoebas are undoubtedly kicking up from the change of climate." Hadn't Teodora been living in Spain? How long had she been in Real del Marqués? And her husband? She had suffered a shock. Not even an earthquake could wake her now. Best that she sleep. How long has she been like this? What are her motives? Who is she afraid of?

"Teodora doesn't lack for reasons." Doña Argenis recounted the events of Teodora's return. "We must respect her wishes. If she wants to hide her presence from Galaor Ucrós, it's no matter of ours. Shush! Let's not let anyone discover her true identity."

At that very moment, the cries of Durango Berrío alerted both owners and guests of the Residencias Argenis.

"Perucho! We won the lottery! We won it! We're millionaires! Big-time! And she's the one who brought us the good luck!"

"And if 'she' is Teodora Vencejos," Doña Argenis's jaws dropped at the thought, "it won't take Galaor Ucrós long to know she's here."

"The later the better," Donado noted. "We can only wait, and trust in God that she'll be fine when she wakes up. She must drink boiled or bottled water. Avoid fits of anger and fried foods. And she must take her remedies religiously." He wrote the prescription in his learned-physician-with-great-experience hand and also recommended broth of dove.

A week later Teodora was still submerged in her strange sleep, from which she emerged only at dusk in order to exist in a different sleep of wide-open eyes and sporadic words. Frightened, Dr. Nemesio Donado sought the help of Don Orígenes Palma, a certified homeopath, who prescribed tincture of calendula, nux vomica, and chamomile drops—without visible effect. What was it? The roots of Teodora's affliction seemed too deep to identify.

On the sly, through the back door, Perucho Cervera and Durango Berrío sneaked in an herbalist, the celebrated Ofir Macaón, who knew how to clear pastures of predators and gallbladders of stones, cure the evil eye and premature impotence, heal bones, and repair damaged maidenheads. To no avail! The man admitted that Teodora Vencejos's illness exceeded his capabilities.

"The poison is self-generated. And my knowledge does not reach so far as a person's soul."

Only Luminosa Palomino, the sister of Visitación, the

María Lionza priestess for all the Atlantic coast, did not hesitate to diagnose: "She's dying of love. Slowly dying."

"And the remedy?"

Luminosa, who had been chosen by the Goddess of Love in her later years and had laboriously learned to read using primers and children's stories—the better to serve María Lionza—spoke in her language of childhood romances.

"The remedy of the Sleeping Beauty in the forest. Only a passionate kiss will awaken her."

"Then we will have to summon Galaor Ucrós," Don Rufino Cervera decreed. "Teodora is in love with that no-good. And that leaves us no choice."

The matter was so thorny, yet so delicate, that Don Rufino Cervera himself crossed the planks to talk with his neighbor. He had wanted to do it in secret, but in the Hotel Ramona they were already alerted because of the reigning commotion over at the Residencias Argenis. The comings and goings of the doctor, the homeopath, the herbalist, and the priestess of María Lionza had upset Clavel Quintanilla, who was again pregnant. She feared that the stranger might have been bitten (as evil gossips had it) by a *machaca*, the killer bee whose venom, in Real del Marqués, was believed to awaken uncontrollable amorous fires, and that in her madness she would set her beautiful eyes on Galaor Ucrós, who was adept at detecting heat from great distances. Galaor, her inconstant, not legitimate, but acceptable husband and father of her children.

"And you, what do you want?" Haughtily, she planted herself before Don Rufino, preventing him from stepping onto the sidewalk or terrace.

"I must speak with Galaor."

"What about?"

"Where can I find him?"

"How do I know? I don't care."

The planks were narrow. Don Rufino Cervera was big and husky, and La Quintanilla was in a snit because Ucrós had escaped the day before and had been seen in the market in hot pursuit of some girls who had just arrived from El Morro—the new Venice—and smelled of fish a kilometer away, and who, with the hip-wiggling and disporting of lacustrine sirens, had stirred up all the womanizers and unredeemed libertines in Real del Marqués.

"Tell him I need to talk with him. It's urgent."

"Me tell him? Tell him what? Go jump in the lake!"

Jealous and never decorous, La Quintanilla began to shuffle her way across the fragile footbridge taxed by neighborhood traffic. Don Rufino Cervera, sweating and corpulent, was sent staggering by a well-placed push from fecund hips. That was when the rotted wood yielded, and both splashed, spectacularly!, into the mud: he like a leaden bear, and she revealing that no underpants could contain her monumental pregnancy.

"Helllup!"

With that dual S.O.S. began the golden age of Real del

Marqués, which would become a spa and vacation center famous for its thermal baths and medicinal mud. For both Clavel Quintanilla and Don Rufino Cervera experienced an immediate improvement in health. Her ills were varicose veins, stretch marks, and a weak bladder. In his case it was a dried-up stalk that no longer rose tall, not even with applications of mentholatum, Chinese ointments, or gringo toothpaste, not even with doses of extract of mandrake or the aphrodisiac *chuchuaza* root—not even with the bite of the *machaca*! For three years he had been unable to make Doña Argenis happy (or nuzzle the neck of the cashier at the American Bar, to say nothing of trying out Lourdes Olea, who worked for Alí Sufyan).

Miraculous mud.

Both would speak with such enthusiasm of their restorative experiences that three weeks later, from every town and city on the Atlantic coast, people came to immerse themselves in the mud and bathe in the thermal waters bubbling up from the subsoil. The Calle de las Camelias was closed to vehicular traffic and its residents granted a special concession to exploit the new wealth, negotiated by the city and state after reaching a just understanding with regard to taxes.

As the mud produced incomparable rejuvenating effects on the bare skin, and the parish priest, Don Imeldo Villamarín, bathed in it every week to ease his arthritis and asthma, the church obtained a percentage of the earnings that quickly began to flow to the benefit, first, of the fortunate proprietors and then the rest of the town.

On one matter, everyone was in agreement. Luck was favoring Real del Marqués. It was said, in low voices, that Teodora Vencejos had expelled that prodigious mud along with her vaginal nectars while levitating in an enchanted and somnambulistic dream of burning legs.

The water was related to the stream of her urine, and the residual clay, perfumed with honey and sold in little pots, to the wax in her ears, or sweat of her armpits, or red of her menstrual flow. With great profit. Although the reality was more pedestrian. Which was that torrential rains and continuous mud slides had uncovered a spring of thermal water hidden beneath layers and layers of kaolin and clay, just beneath the foundations of the Residencias Argenis.

So who cared about the truth? Who? Luck had come to Real del Marqués, perhaps following the footsteps of Teodora Vencejos. Perhaps. So no one pursued the matter of the kiss. Who was going to awaken her? Who had the right?

Galaor Ucrós? No way. His behavior to Teodora had diminished him in the eyes of his neighbors, and neither was he interested in functioning as prince consort. Why tie a rope around his own neck? And wake his legitimate wife? He had problems enough with the Other Woman, La Quintanilla, with his new lover, and with the demanding nieces of Leocadia Payares. Wake Teodora? All right. He would. Sure, of course. First, though, he had to lose his beer belly, clean up the Hotel Ramona, and get his older daughters, Demetria and Esmaracola, in school and under control. He would have to throw out his comfort-loving father-in-law and enterprising mother-in-law, but how? Teodora awake and dedicated to work was one thing. If she announced a visit to her family, the in-laws would be off at a run. It was something else if she kept sleeping away in the house across the street. Galaor found her illness convenient. There would always be people to take care of her: Doña Argenis and Perucho Cervera; Visitación Palomino; Roseta Alvira, the seamstress; Lourdes Olea, Alí Sufyan's faithful employee; Hada Reales from the American Bar; even the priestess of María Lionza—called Luminosa and baptized Nacar Blondina, despite being as inky black as her sister. And always, Zulema Sufyan.

Each of them had powerful reasons—besides their affection—to care for the sleeping woman and to guard her like a fabulous treasure. Doña Argenis, because her residence had been transformed into a high-priced hotel and, above and beyond that, because she had in her bed a fiery and faithful husband. Perucho, because he was no longer the kid of the family; thanks to the lottery, he was worth millions. Roseta Alvira, because she had left her sewing machine and underpaid hours behind and was designing merry Bermuda shorts for the tourists. Visitación Palomino was more thrilled than anyone. Her better half, her black Natanael

Osías, who had run off five years before with a merengue singer, was back with his tail between his legs, abruptly abandoned on the very day Luminosa had said, "Teodora Vencejos is dying of love."

Durango Berrío had reasons to spare. He was rich and respected; he was providing a good life to his wife and children; he had a much improved smile, perfect teeth, and a transport business. Happiest of all, however, were Lourdes Olea and Hada Reales, who had opened a beer parlor and dedicated themselves 100 percent to flirtation, for both had wasted their youth behind counters and cash registers, and their appetite for handsome young men still robbed them of sleep and warmed their splendid pudendas.

Yes, everyone had reasons for looking after the sleeping beauty. But no one knew the specific source of Zulema's concern for Teodora, and no one could have imagined. It was she who began to pester her husband with an obsessive idea.

"You have to find Dr. Amiel, or Teodora will lie asleep all her life."

"Find thee dok-tor. And vere?"

"Wherever he is."

"An' you, my qveen. Vy do you care, blease?"

"Why should I know? You have to call him and beg him to come back."

"You want I should televon Europes? You are crazy, blease? Is mucho expansive, voman. You, you vish ruin modest man? Honorable businessman, vat you thinging, blease?"

Alí Sufyan was growing rich from the sale of towels, dresses, bathrobes, dark glasses, and related articles. Later he would emerge as the continental czar of thong bikinis, whose advertising edicts would carry him to the highest peaks of the business world.

"Don't be so tightfisted."

Zulema stuck to her guns. She knew why, but did not want to tell anyone her reasons. When the Turk (who in fact was Arab) asked her, "Vy? Vy so inderested in Teodora?" she replied, "I know what I know."

Alí, who still had hidden guilt feelings from the first year of his marriage, agreed to place a call to Spain. As the house-keeper informed him that Dr. Amiel was on a trip, opening markets for his most successful products (the lotion Aflame, tamarind sweets, fried ants whose disproportionate posteriors promised prodigious prowess, *machaca* tails with magical stingers, salt-and-peppered palm fruit—as well as edible panties and feathers for tickling), Alí was forced to place call after call before locating Amiel in a sauna in Manila. Just as six girls with almond-shaped eyes were licking and nibbling at the masque he had created of aloe, mint, beaten partridge eggs, and aphrodisiac cardamom liquors and rubbed over a body tormented by the prolonged absence of Teodora Vencejos.

"Tell whoever it is that I'm not here. I left on a trip."

JOY AND JUBILATION

The day that Teodora Vencejos argued so bitterly with Dr. Amiel, she found she had hours to herself, free of the catering service, hors d'oeuvres, essences, and domestic chores. Radiant, idle, mistress of the fresh air and the first bus. But, as all roads lead to Rome—in her case symbolized by Real del Marqués, its plaza and its modest church—she finally succumbed to routine. She found it sensible, natural, to go by the parish house. Sunday after Sunday, following early mass, Padre Imeldo Villamarín had said to her: "I need to talk with you, my child. To free you from a promise."

Teodora paid not the least attention. She had been too busy with her cakes, her mamey and plum sweets, the activities of keeping her house and looking after young Galaor.

What a coincidence! It was almost as if the priest had been waiting for her. He did not evince any delight at her unexpected visit or shower her with pleasantries. He looked worried, his eyes veiled with sadness and a far distant hope.

"How long has Galaor Ucrós been back living under your roof?" he asked.

Sitting in a wicker rocking chair, wrapped in a white cassock and holding a large book in his slender hands, he seemed very fragile.

"Oh, two weeks or more. I don't remember exactly. Maybe a month? Isn't it a blessing, Padre?"

"I don't believe in that kind of blessing. Where is your head, girl? Don't you have any regard for your good name?" And he stroked the medallion of the Virgin of Eternal Succor he wore around his emaciated neck.

"What are you trying to say, Padre?"

"Galaor Ucrós is a grown man, not a babe at the teat. You, on the other hand, are in the flower of your youth. It is not appropriate for you to live with him under the same roof. Such an arrangement scandalizes simple people. It serves to feed gossip."

"I haven't even seen him," Teodora protested. "All I want to do is wash his clothes and prepare his food. My madrina Ramonita commended him to me on her deathbed."

Padre Imeldo Villamarín jumped up from his rocker. With shortened, listing steps he approached the console table crowded with large iridescent bottles, liquors, and jams labeled in Dr. Amiel's hand.

"I heard every confession Ramona Céspedes de Ucrós

ever made," he said, pouring anisette into two glasses, a little for Teodora and quite a lot for himself. "I knew the soul of your madrina inside and out. Which is why I feel I have the authority to command you to forget your promises! I absolve you in the name of God. From purgatory your godmother will, I feel sure, be grateful to you."

"Can you do that, Padre Imeldo? Are you sure?" Teodora could not believe the possibility of such joy and jubilation. If Galaor was no longer in her care, if he was not forbidden to her, maybe he would look on her as a woman.

"Who else could have the power? My authority comes from on high. I am a priest, the head of a church, God's minister on earth. You understand?"

"Thank you, Padre Imeldo. I understand, and I am very grateful to you."

"Don't be grateful to me. Get Galaor Ucrós out of your house. Immediately!"

"That I can't do."

"You must. You are not bound by any promise. You are free."

"I will not throw young Galaor from the house of his ancestors. Never. I would rather go myself."

"Listen, my child, you have no obligation to him. As Catón Nieto told you, the house is yours. Along with all the rest. Galaor has blown his inheritance and will make his way through yours, if you don't look sharp."

"What are you insinuating, Padre?"

"Beware a Christ heavy with silver, girl!"

Wasted time. Padre Imeldo could not reason with Teodora, who, without tasting her anisette, seized her pocketbook and ran to the door. And as she left, raised her voice, as if challenging a deaf priest.

"Galaor Ucrós is my true inheritance. That is enough for me."

Besides the anisette, Padre Imeldo Villamarín drank a bottle of brandy.

Definitely—Teodora decided then and there—she would look after herself. She would cook and bake in the large kitchen of her house, and to avoid evil gossip she would hire an assistant and utilize the services of Peruchito Cervera and Asisclo Alandete as delivery boys. She would go farther! For a laughable sum, she would rent out her extra rooms to decent working girls like Lourdes Olea, Roseta Alvira, and Hada Reales, who would live in them, without kitchen privileges. Yes, that is what she would do. And that depraved Dr. Amiel could go to the Devil!

As she entered the house, she was so absorbed in her thoughts that she failed to notice Galaor until she found herself locked in his muscular embrace. She inhaled his mentholated breath, the scent of French cologne, the clean fragrance of the nightshirt she herself had washed, and the smell of a young man on his way from an unmade bed to a cold shower, which she in her innocence confused with the perfume of the angels in heaven.

"Teodora, my beloved. How happy I am to see you! I think of you, dream of you, every day." His lips on her lips, his tongue seeking her teeth, feverishly licking her eyelids and delicate ears.

"Galaor, for God's sake, be sensible."

"Whatever you say."

Respectfully, Galaor put his arm around Teodora's waist. Gentle, tender. As if several days before he had invited her for a walk, and this were a long awaited rendezvous. Immersed in the spell of his fine-spun mustache, his warm kisses, his velvety voice, Teodora heard words spill from her lips: her promise to Doña Ramonita, the dispensation Padre Imeldo had given her, and the decisions she had made to short-circuit gossip and free herself of the tyranny of Dr. Amiel. While Galaor devoured her with blue eyes swimming with lavish promises.

"None of this renting out rooms. What an idea! And give up your job? That's madness."

"There's no other way."

"There is. The most beautiful of remedies. The blessing of blessings. We'll get married!"

He told her that no woman—not Copelia Arantza, not La Quintanilla, not the Del Rosal sisters, not the false nieces of Leocadia Payares—meant anything to him, anything at all. Living beneath the same roof and having grown up by Teodora's side had prevented him from expressing his tenderest feelings. But fate, in its infinite wisdom, had schemed to thwart his marriage to a stranger. And why? Because they were destined for each other, that's why; it was time they accepted it. They must join together body and soul, breathe the same air, sleep upon the same pillow, be drenched by the same rain, walk to the same rhythm, share for richer, for poorer. The one thing he asked, he said, as his hand crept up her firm thighs, explored between her panties and feathery black curls, was the most absolute secrecy. Neither he nor Teodora must say a word to anyone. At least until the echoes of his unfortunate liaison with the oldest Arantza sister died down.

"Agreed?"

Teodora did not respond, prisoner as she was to the music, the sound, the magic of those words, to the spellbinding smile Galaor directed only at her, and the kisses curving beneath the wheat of his blond mustache. Lower down, the trembling petals of her fragrant chrysanthemum opened and grew moist, offering itself with passionate ardor.

"Do you promise?"

Teodora thought she was dying. She was skin and pores and sinuosities starving for those hands, those caresses, that other skin, that submissive tongue—that breech-loader that could not fire for lack of ammunition.

"If that's what you want, yes."

Whereas other women have sparks of intuition, sense on the clothing of their beloved the presence of possible lovers, and die of jealousy for feelings as yet unborn, Teodora Vencejos suffered absolute blindness. It never occurred to her to believe or to suspect that Clavel Quintanilla had just left through the back door. Or that Galaor had no strength remaining to advance, occupy the besieged citadel, bury his pike in Flanders.

"Ayyyy, yes, yes! YES!"

"No," he said. "You are my future wife. We will wait until our wedding night."

CLOAKS, HOODS, AND VEILS

During her prolonged sleep, Teodora's hair grew sumptuously, night after night, and it was necessary to cut a hand's span a week to keep her from entangling herself in it when she got out of bed. Besides washing and brushing what she had cut, Zulema Sufyan—who also filed Teodora's finger and toenails—gathered handfuls of curls for Luminosa Palomino to give to impotent husbands and lovers overwhelmed by jealousy, hopelessness, or possessiveness. Locks wrapped in small leather or velvet pouches to be worn next to the skin. With miraculous effects! Zulema herself, when she had despaired of having a child, had conceived twins after braiding a ring for Alí from Teodora's pubic hair. Terrified of hearing the "I divorce you, I divorce you, I divorce you" at the discretion of the followers of Muhammad.

How could she abandon Teodora in her misfortune? That was the question tormenting the happy wife of Alí Sufyan. Before long, during the first weeks following the birth, she would have to leave her. And friends of the sleeping woman had tried in vain to find Dr. Manuel Amiel. What to do? Zulema pleaded with Luminosa Palomino to exercise all her esoteric arts, even to seek the aid of all her fellow sorceresses of the Atlantic coast, herb gatherers, diviners, and mind readers, so that with their combined powers they could attract the evasive entrepreneur/chef (wherever he might be) or any other man who might break the awesome lethargy into which Teodora Vencejos had fallen with the revelation of the truth.

Zulema wanted to give birth without anxiety and to prevent Alí's asking too many questions about her obvious devotion to Teodora. If her friend returned to normality, and happiness presided over the birth, she would have nothing to fear. Otherwise, however, she would have to avoid the subject, or lie, or, much worse, invent a story that would not hold up. Because there was no way she would tell the true story of how she had won the love of a husband she had wed in an arranged marriage.

Above all, she could not permit him to ask questions in the name of the Prophet or of his blessed wives.

When Alí Sufyan began looking for a bride, he had been offered several girls from his native land—Aminas and Aifas and Farides—who would bring with them substantial dowries that were truly tempting for a sagacious merchant and worshipper of money. But they were girls who lived on the other side of the world in cities like Damascus, Medina, or Aden, or in the Dahana or Kaf deserts, whom he could know only through photographs. He might contract to marry a virginal damsel escaped from Paradise or a tub of flesh otherwise condemned to spinsterhood. In either case, he would have to teach her Spanish, how to eat, dress, and love a new country, how to establish relationships and help him in a thriving business. So he began to look around among the sisters and daughters of his countrymen. A girl born locally would be preferable, one not given to ennui or nostalgia. That seemed the most prudent course for a man like himself, who wanted to treat his wife as an equal. And in that regard, he had on the tip of his tongue a phrase he had heard Dr. Amiel use, and that he never learned had come from the Talmud and not the Koran: "God avoided creating woman from the feet of man, in order that he not tread upon her; from the brain of man, that he not be surpassed by her. He created her from a rib that they might be equals." And Alí added that inside the human breast beat the heart.

He had seen Zulema Essad, a jeweler's daughter, behind an elegant shop counter in Barranquilla. And it was not difficult to gain permission to call upon her every week when he asked for her hand. Good catches like himself, well off and of Arab descent, were few and far between. Besides, Zulema had always looked on him with favor.

"A handsome pair," as Doña Argenis and Don Rufino Cervera would say when they were invited to the wedding dinner.

Alí and Zulema were married after six months' courtship, in a circumspect civil ceremony; more than three hundred guests attended the reception in the Club Arabe. Up to that point, Eden. However, neither Zulema Essad nor Alí Sufyan was to know the "fey state," the mad happiness that according to Arabs augurs inevitable disaster; following their wedding ceremony, they proceeded directly to the latter. Which continued without letup or attenuation. For Alí, accustomed to the ways of La Payares and her purported nieces, found himself unable to touch a woman given him in the name of the prophet Muhammad. Before her he stood mute, frozen. Neither his muscles, his mind, nor his heart responded.

A stranger in Real del Marqués, not knowing in whom to confide, Zulema had noted the admiration her husband felt for Teodora Vencejos. When he thought no one was watching, he used to follow her with his eyes, and he always called her the 'barfect voman.'" It was to Teodora, in an act of desperation, that Zulema went for counsel, dissolved in tears, on the eve of Carnival.

"Help me!" she begged.

"Me? What can I do?"

"Teach me how to win over my husband."

"Me?"

"Tell me whom to turn to. Tell me whether I can trust in you. Teach me the way."

Teodora already had the responsibility of her girls, Demetria and Esmaracola, and did not know much about love. She opted for the most direct course: to visit Luminosa Palomino, who was by then serving María Lionza and was famous for her knowledge of herbs, baths, incense, philtres, potions, and talismans. From her Teodora would learn to mix diosma with artemesia and cinnamon; *limonaria* with jasmine and verbena; orange blossoms with violets and the bark of the *anamú*; myrtle with mint and calendulas. A wide range of flowers, fruits, roots, and twigs that later Dr. Amiel would use to benefit many as he collected, one by one, the debts Teodora had run up with him.

"You can help her," said Luminosa. "You were born with the gift of love and fertility. Do not forsake her. She will bathe seven times, seven days, in cinnamon water, roses, and orange leaves. Then three times, three days, with verbena, sweet basil, and heliotrope. And rinse with sugar water. The rest I leave to your knowledge and understanding. You can do it! Today for you, tomorrow for me, do not forget. One day you will have need of Zulema Sufyan. I see it in the air."

Teodora, who was a simple woman, decided to trust in the words of Dr. Amiel. "Love is a tyrant, and to please him many, many rules have been broken." So she asked Zulema: "What do you suggest? I don't have any ideas."

"Alí is enchanted with you. If you are me and I am you, he will think we're the same. As I am his wife, he will have affection for me."

"What shall we do?"

They went to Barranquilla and bought two identical black, hooded, and veiled capes with red trim, and two pairs of gold slippers, one with higher heels for Zulema, who even on tiptoes came only to Teodora's shoulder.

"We must smell the same," said La Essad-Sufyan.

So they bathed in the same infusions of herbs and flowers, rubbed their bodies with essence of rose and cinnamon, and in their hooded and veiled cloaks ran to mix with the revelers who packed the American Bar, now converted into a dance floor for the occasion of Carnival.

"Alí . . . darling Alí Sufyan."

From the first night, the Turk (who in truth was Arab) was pursued by a mysterious admirer in beautiful gold slippers, who apparently wore nothing beneath the cloth of her cape.

"Alíííí, beloved."

The woman's aroma, the possibility of the naked body, the red-lacquered toenails, maddened Sufyan, who could not stop murmuring as they danced fiery boleros: "Just like Teodora you smell!"

Of course, Alí immediately desired the cloaked woman. Hour after hour, his yearning grew, boiling into an unrestrained passion that could lead to only one ending. Being together, naked, in a motel on the coast highway, to make love that surpassed delirium itself.

"Tell me, yes, blease! You other barfect voman."

But as they made their way among the other dancers, the caped woman slipped away and faded into a dance swirling in front of the American Bar. Toom, tatoom, baroooom. Amid trumpets, flutes, and drums, Alí pursued his own wife, unidentifiable beneath the black cape with red trim.

"Come vid me. Blease!" As he turned the corner, he seized the arm of Teodora Vencejos.

She, her hood and veil carefully in place, dictated her conditions. Never for any reason must he try to find out who she was or where she was from. He must never ask her name. The reason was simple to divine. She was wildly in love with Alí Sufyan, but she was a married woman. And she could not give cause for talk, or embarrass her husband. And she could not—she announced—give herself completely. He must not abuse her conditions.

Alí Sufyan swore by his mother, by the homeland of his ancestors, by the desert of the Sahara and the soul of the prophet Muhammad, whose holiness did not prevent his having a soft spot for women.

White, cool, soft as butter. Perfumed with herbs, cinnamon, and roses, the mysterious caped woman allowed Alí to caress her body slowly but not remove the silk teddy that smelled like Teodora Vencejos. She opened her legs to allow him to tongue her flower, petal by petal, her pistil, corolla, and nectar. Although she did not allow him to enter.

"Eggsactly like Teodora," murmured Alí. "Isss her aroma."

Back home, Zulema smelled exactly like Teodora to him, like his capricious lover. Near frenzy, he tried to make love to his wife, who despite having sworn obedience to the ways of Islam, did not want to give her body to a husband who had gone out to rhumba at dusk and not returned until after daybreak.

Angry, Alí returned to the fiesta on Saturday of Carnival and found his beloved waiting for him at the doors to the American Bar. Again they danced, bodies pressed tightly together, his leg between hers, member against mound, breath to breath. Of the desired woman he could see only the feet in the gold sandals gleaming in the light of the street lamps. Bound by an oath, he did not open his lips to ask questions or capitulations.

He murmured only, "Eggsactly like Zulema you smell."

It was she, again, who danced with Alí until dawn, then fled, fading into the crowd, allowing Teodora to take her place at the critical moment. And that night, gazing at Alí with sad eyes, the hooded and veiled woman called an end to the romance. They were in danger, she said; they could not go on. Theirs was an impossible love; her husband, a jealous man, was growing suspicious. They must say good-bye.

It was good-bye forever and ever. Unbearable! Thus, as a last concession, she allowed Alí to place his banana between her breasts, possess her armpits, and rub his semen on her belly. No "blease," no "ayys," no promises could induce her to allow him to enter the tunnel of her rose. She did not want to give to a stranger what she had dedicated to another in holy wedlock.

"Then vy you unfaidvul, blease?"

The reply of the adored woman in the cape stopped the heart of Alí Sufyan.

"What will be eaten by worms is best enjoyed by Christians. My husband prefers other women, he does not want to touch me, he does not fancy me. What is there for me to do?"

The burning night of love Alí Sufyan had promised himself abruptly changed to nightmare. A warrior's blood exploded like dynamite in his frozen veins. He did not even kiss the stranger as he left. He was in a frenzy to know. Was Zulema at home? In her bedroom in her own bed? Or was she somewhere out there, running after the first man who bestirred himself to make love to her?

On his way home, Alí bought three bottles of the best champagne, for although Muhammad had forbidden wine, he had never mentioned a word about champagne, and in the name of love many sins against the Koran are pardoned.

What relief! Zulema was curled up in bed in a simple gown, her eyes filled with tears, but she smelled like the

houri of Paradise. For a fleeting moment, Alí Sufyan had a
bad thought.

"Just the same as Teodora!"

But it lasted only an instant, like an acetylene spark, and
just as quickly it vanished. Zulema was his wife, of his people,
with the same customs, and the best cook in Barranquilla's
Arab colony. Her tahini made him smack his lips. To say nothing of her kibbi, her almond sweets, her couscous. She was
beautiful, submissive, and did not go out dancing in capes,
like some other women, to open her thighs to the first man
who laid a hand on her and told her how beautiful her eyes
were.

"I vant beg you pardon, blease. You my vife, barfect
voman, morning star, you spring of cool vater. I do vat my
prancess tell me. I give many pretties to my love."

"I want nothing."

"Nutding?"

Poor Alí Sufyan was being pushed uphill by life. Zulema
made him beg and plead.

"Vat you vish, blease, my bride?"

"A cloak. I want to go out dancing with you."

"Am-possibul! Nutding more you vant, blease?"

"Nothing."

"New dress?"

"No."

"New auto?"

"No."

As it turned out, Zulema became the first "Turk" in Real del Marqués to accompany her husband dancing, without a veil, in the American Bar, in the Club Seferides, and at the Arte and the Sabor, after making love one whole Carnival Sunday and melting forever Alí's indifference—at a premium! And she would have accepted nothing. Nevertheless, as he wanted to compensate her, Zulema left her bed with the world on a silver platter. A new house for a few kisses above her calves; stock in the Club Campestre for fingering her husband's fiddle; the latest-model car for kissing, slowly, ever more slowly, the center and surrounding areas of his plump stomach; and a trip to Europe when he galloped into the virginal palace, spattering the sheets with young, red, healthy blood, as the passion, the longing, the shadow of Teodora Vencejos evaporated . . . and the purported nieces of Leocadia Payares lost, forever and all time, one of their best clients.

Zulema Sufyan would never tell the truth to anyone, not even if they stoned her. Yet she was not ready to allow her best friend to wander forever in a limbo devoid of love and passion and memory. She, Zulema, was near to bringing into the world a son of Islam, and the spiritual force was with her. Now she did not even fear the laws of her ancestors! Better for Alí to walk the straight and narrow. He was not the only one who could call on divorce if things did not go his way.

"I want Teodora Vencejos to be the godmother to my son, or he will be a child without a name!"

The question of the godmother was like the champagne. Muhammad had said nothing against it. Alí tried to obey the laws of the Koran, but Zulema was a Barranquilla woman baptized in the Catholic Church and married in a mixed ceremony conducted by Catón Nieto. Alí saw nothing wrong in offering a huge fiesta when the boy—or boys— were taken to the civil registry. That was not condemned by any Sura of the Koran. None. So Zulema stood firm in her demands.

"I must have Teodora recover her reason. We must locate Dr. Amiel."

HAVE MERCY ON ME!

Early the next morning, bursting with happiness, Teodora
decided to visit Padre Imeldo Villamarín. She wanted him to
be the first mortal to hear the marvelous news of her wedding and to erase all the reproaches that appeared in the
priest's eyes when they exchanged a "Buenos días" or
"Buenas tardes." She was humming to herself, her future
pleasure tickling the orifices and curves of her body.

"I'm getting married. I'm getting married married married. Married, Teodora and Galaor."

Against the text and the subtext of that melody without
music rose a scene created in the dawn of her virginal
insomnia. Don Imeldo Villamarín, ramrod straight in his
gold-bordered white satin chasuble, his hand tracing a cross
in the air, was saying before a church filled with Real del

Marquesians: "I declare you husband and wife. Now, Galaor Ucrós, you may kiss the bride."

Anything that preceded that blessed instant had no substance in her thoughts and eluded capture as tone, color, sound, even human form. The priest's words, therefore, came like a rock shattering the crystal bell protecting the delicate structure of her daydream.

"I freed you from a promise, and you choose to crucify yourself. Where are your brains, girl? Do you think with your head or your behind? Wake up! You remember the saying, It may not be much, but at least it's all mine? You can't even say that about Galaor Ucrós!"

"I don't understand, Padre."

"Either you are hopelessly stupid or you've lost your senses. I would not marry you to that imbecile if I were guaranteed a crown in the Kingdom of Heaven. Now get out of here! If you don't, I'm going to turn you over my knee and paddle you. And may Don Martiniano Vencejos forgive me for laying a hand on a daughter of his. Blessed be his soul!"

"I'm getting married anyway." Teodora did not seem like Teodora.

"Over my dead body." And while he was rolling up his sleeves to whip off his belt, Don Imeldo thought he heard the thunderous voice of the departed Martiniano, urging him to "lay it on her, Padre. Hard!"

The popular saying goes that love thrives under duress,

and that phrase consoled a saddened Teodora in her long trek through the churches of Barranquilla, Caracolí, Sabanalarga, Malambo, and Arroyo de Piedra, where she was met with successive refusals. Ringing nos that admitted no possibility of appeal hovered in all the offices of all the parishes of Atlántico, Bolívar, El Magdalena, and perhaps the rest of the country. The circular that forbade parish priests to celebrate the marriage of Señorita Teodora Vencejos and Galaor Ucrós was signed by the archbishop himself, the primate of Bogotá, a seminary classmate of Padre Imeldo's and a close personal friend. No specific reasons were given, but anyone who knew how to read between the lines could not miss the skillfully interjected fear of incest. "The Ministers of the Church shall abstain from imparting a blessing upon the projected union of our beloved children in Christ, Galaor Ucrós de Céspedes and Teodora Vencejos Arraut, so long as said near brother and sister do not first live for one year beneath different roofs, thereby demonstrating that a solid basis exists for said union, as well as their willingness to fulfill the mandates of the Holy Mother Church."

According to the opinion of counselor Catón Nieto, a specialist in family law, such a proceeding had no juridical validity. It could be reversed. And did they have the money to file a complaint? Were they prepared to quarrel with the Curia? It was not worth the price. Nor did Galaor have any intention of moving, anyway, since his inheritance had evaporated during the period of his mourning, his sadness and indecision, and his onerous courtship with La Arantza. And especially not now while he was wavering between a marriage of convenience and one of true love.

As the finishing touch, Teodora was not able to store away a single sheet, handkerchief, or napkin—say nothing of lingerie—for her trousseau. Her credit was exhausted. Her friends in Real del Marqués were visibly slipping away, just when she needed them most.

"No," Alí Sufyan told her. "I not charge you undervear. That man not vorthy of prancess, and my relijohn say not fool vid destiny."

Lourdes Olea, who dealt in smuggled merchandise, apparently behind the Turk's back—although in fact with his financing—saw an opportunity to score a small revenge. She still sighed over Galaor Ucrós, with whom she had danced three nights in a row during the festivals and street dancing that preceded Carnival. She sighed . . . Those hands clasping her hips and exploring her breasts beneath her blouse, his right leg between hers and that expert knee thrilling her thighs as they danced, the frisky phallus against her waist, her navel, the line of fuzz that divided his stomach and languished toward the groin. And suddenly, that ice cream cone she had cherished would—every last sweet morsel—be all for that fat-assed, big-titted Teodora Vencejos. Too much! An insult! She, Lourdes Olea, whom all the regulars at the American Bar called "The Breeze," for her way of walking, had not had so much as a tiny taste. Massaged, excited, touched "down there," she was still as virgin as the day her mother brought her into the world.

She could never let her have silk on credit, Lourdes told Teodora. It was too big a risk. Still, she had beautiful items in delicate cotton from India. With fine lace, little rosettes, hemstitching, satin ribbons, and silk embroidery. Those were the undergarments preferred by the best young girls: sweet sixteens, debutantes, bashful new brides. Angelic, but with a sexy touch that offended no one.

"Galaor, being such a gentleman, and so respectful, will like them," commented Teodora.

Lourdes Olea failed to warn her that those garments were not fit to be sold, and that she had two full drawers of them. A white, almost transparent moth had infested the delicate cotton and had already eaten entire shipments of briefs and girdles and brassieres and petticoats. The tiny eggs deposited in the seams and rosettes resisted sprays, mothballs, and hot irons but erupted as soon as they felt the heat of bare skin.

The lingerie was a lost investment. Lourdes wanted to keep her elegant clients and the favor of daughters of the best families. But Teodora did not fit into those categories, and who complains about articles bought on credit? She just hoped the insects would devour that ingrate Galaor's famous golden rod.

That cotton lingerie would be the only luxury Teodora

could claim on the day of her civil wedding. Roseta, the seamstress, had refused to make her a bridal gown.

"Not on credit, not as a gift, not paid in full," she said defiantly, crying so hard her nose ran. "I would never do anything that bad to you. Not you, my dear, dear friend."

"Do bad? Bad? What are you talking about? I am immensely happy."

"Happy or miserable, don't say I didn't warn you. And why marry him? A woman like you is worth your weight in gold dust and polished emeralds. She doesn't throw herself at a pretty mustache. That handsome philanderer is not worth the dirt you walk on. Are you that crazy to crawl into bed with someone? Better to have a fling with one of the *bogas* who paddle their produce to the market and give yourself a good time. You'd come out ahead."

Teodora's heart ached as she left the seamstress's house. Little Roseta. So thin, so spindly, and glasses to boot. She was dying of envy!

It went no better with Visitación Palomino when Teodora tried to order food for the wedding dinner. The black face split into a sarcastic grin.

"You want a big feast for your wedding, right? I'd suggest, maybe, pigs' feet and *arroz con pollo*. Maybe turkey stuffed with tomato salad and green papaya? Or rice with coconut and a *posta negra* beef roast? No! Oh! Then snails, and rice with *chipichipi*, and those honey-and-clove *platanitos*? Or maybe we should serve baked porgy, and rice with raisins, and kidneys in wine? Or even sautéed *mojarras* with *patacones* would be tasty. So, Niña Teodora, is that what you had in mind?"

"The rice and coconut, the roast, and pigs' feet would be enough. And the *platanitos pícaros* as a dessert. I'm not going to invite many people."

Visitación Palomino stood squarely with her hands on her hips in a martial pose she had learned in other times, when she was cooking for the army and head-over-heels in love with her black Natanael, then a handsome corporal.

"You're not even warm, Teodora, my girl. I will not throw a single garlic bud, or a cumin or dill seed, into the pot. Not one pinch of salt. So you can marry that high-lifer. Not me. And when are you going to pay me what you owe me? With the money from the IOU's Don Galaor Ucrós signed, I could have got myself a twenty-year-old stud and bought me a bed worthy of the king himself, Muhammad Ali—if it's to be my destiny to support a man."

"IOUs? Galaor? When? For what? In my house, I'm the cook."

"But in the paramour's house, the fire's never lit. Garlic and onion give Clavel Quintanilla nausea and colic. They say she's pregnant again."

Teodora returned home sobbing like Mary Magdalene. Galaor Ucrós, who was settling in for a siesta in his hammock, had to devote nearly an hour, and a lot of soothing talk, to calming the fears that paralyzed his beloved, his childhood sister, and his future wife—not to discount the hands that never paused for a moment.

"People are so mean. And envious! They can't stand for anyone else to be happy, they want us to be miserable. Paramour? When have I ever kept a paramour? I may have had a flirtation or two, nothing of any importance. And one formal sweetheart, who made a fool out of me."

Into her ear, he whispered, "You're my baby doll, my love, my sugar bud, my plump little pudding, my treasure, my darling heart," although the narrowness of the hammock limited him to nothing more than stroking her legs, touching her earlobe with his tongue, and snuggling his nose between her breasts. Just as well he could go no farther, because even had the invader's cannon tried to enter Rome, it would stubbornly have refused to fire. Clavel Quintanilla had burned all the powder the night before.

"We must be married right away!" he said. "It's the only way to stamp out the rumors."

Teodora contended that they hadn't set the month or day or time. And she didn't have her trousseau ready, or her dress, or preparations for the party. Not even friends to invite.

"So what? With our great love, we'll have everything we need and love left over. We'll have a civil service."

Love was not enough to break the hateful silence that clung to Teodora's footsteps when she walked down Calle de las Camelias on the way to church or the market. Only Peruchito Cervera—the innocent!—dared defy the wrath of

Doña Argenis. He blew her kisses from his fingertips and on paper airplanes, brought her bottles of watermelon, guava, and raspberry soda, not to mention ice cream and huge molasses cookies.

"If I were big!" he used to say in his flutey little voice.

Even in the market, where a few simple people still let her buy sugar, *panelas*, candied fruit, fresh eggs, and flour on credit, the atmosphere was growing poisonous. Whispers snaked through the stands of foodstuffs and the fish and chicken and meat stalls. Even the *bogas* who came from upriver and the new Venice to sell *yuca*, *ñame*, and plantains had something to say about "la señá Teodora." And cruel stories made the rounds: that she transmitted an illness that robbed a man of his taste for food but enlivened a woman's; that men became overly demanding with their wives and wanted to honeysuckle morning, afternoon, and night; that naive young girls went out in the street lifting their skirts to anyone, because of the essences and liquors put in their cakes and flans; that after seeing her, innocent young boys spent the whole day pinching fannies.

And the *bogas* went back home singing:

> *Señ'ita Teodora, give me some*
>   *more'a,*
> *Señ'ita mine, tell me the time,*
> *Señ'ita Missus, give me some*
>   *kisses,*
> *then put your hand lower.*
> *Have mercy on me!*

And they rushed their wives off to camp beds and cots, strutting, feeling they were the last word in fancy dancing.

Resigned, Teodora lost her creditors and customers one by one. Almost no one in Real del Marqués asked for her culinary services anymore. Or in Barranquilla; after Dr. Amiel left and closed his cafés, few people asked for her delicacies. Men, for fear that their requests would be rejected by Amiel's modest employee. Women, because they dreaded any hint of scandal, of being lumped with Bedelia Afanador, once a highly virtuous lady, who besides living quite openly with the owner of the Suavecito Bar, had the gall to parade herself with him—in a convertible the color of a baby chick—eternally pregnant and wearing a happy smile from ear to ear.

Resigned, also, to delaying her painfully desired wedding (and the blessing of Padre Imeldo), Teodora changed her mind when she heard Peruchito humming one of the many ditties circulating behind her back. No time to lose! She must marry as soon as possible. If not, she, Teodora Vencejos Arraut, the only daughter of the greatly respected Don Martiniano and goddaughter of Doña Ramonita, would leave Real del Marqués amidst the jeers of an entire town. No time to lose! Even if the church bells weren't ringing.

BELOVED WOMAN

In two weeks' time, Alí Sufyan had spent a fortune in tele-grams, faxes, telephone calls, and express-mail letters. And despite having worked out an advantageous agreement with the state-owned communications company and obtain-ing acceptable discounts, his good humor was beginning to turn to irritation. He was suffering palpitations, dizzy spells, intermittent rashes. The milk in his coffee tasted sour, the mint in the kibbi bitter, the tahini, watery. He was incapable of offending or disappointing his beautiful Zulema, yet nei-ther did he want to toss money into the air. And the only person who could stop the flow of money invested in the laborious search was Dr. Amiel himself.

"What if he doesn't come?" Zulema asked herself. "What will become of my life? What will happen to Teodora?"

As it was not advisable to abandon the matter entirely to

the communications company, and following the counsel of Doña Argenis Cervera, Zulema asked Alí's permission to summon Luminosa Palomino for aid and assistance. The Turk (actually, Arab) was so desperate that he allowed his legitimate wife to involve herself in infidel practices. "May Allah forgive them!" After all, the prophet Muhammad, so respected by men and loved by women, had never needed the protection of a María Lionza to achieve his goals, and after all, wasn't the Goddess of Love a product of the New World, of obscure religions, and the imaginings of people who did not even know in what direction the sacred city of Mecca lay?

"If it be your command, Allah, strike me dead vid lidtning. So it be, blease!"

As Allah remained silent, Zulema advanced Luminosa Palomino enough money to assure her best efforts and waited seven days and seven nights for the priestess to leave her house one crack of dawn, laden with the necessary philtres, ointments, sprays, and lucky stones. Silently, with furtive steps, to prevent her vital energies from evaporating in a Real del Marqués atmosphere heavy with the breath and humors of residents and tourists. Above all, steadfast in her devotion to María Lionza, for Luminosa's goal was to stop Teodora Vencejos from traveling indefinitely along the path of a circular dream in which it was not easy to find a rift to facilitate her return.

It was as if Luminosa Palomino were navigating through

Teodora's mind and spirit. And Teodora, who most of the time had lived in Madrid as a castaway lives on an island, was slowly walking backward within time that now could never be happy even in memory and was, furthermore, beyond recovery. In that twilight zone it was noon, in autumn; she did not have a friend she could telephone or a child waiting for his treat of *panelitas de leche* or *espejuelo de guanábana* candy. She did not know the bars on her block or the name of the baker or butcher or fishmonger, and she had never even said hello to the youth who tended the shop with dried fruit. Go to the movies or the theater? Not a chance. She had spent months and years working to support Galaor and the girls, whom she considered her own daughters, saving every last peseta. Not allowing herself an ice cream, a section of sugarcane, or a handful of toasted seeds when she went for her Sunday walk to feed the fish and the doves in the Parque del Retiro.

Where, in her return to the past, was she going? She would be sending an urgent telegram to Colombia, to Real del Marqués, the text of which she had written on several occasions: SOLEDAD AIRPORT. I ARRIVE SATURDAY NIGHT. FLIGHT 357 AVIANCA. WITH DEEPEST LOVE. TEODORA.

From the other side of the ocean would come Clavel Quintanilla's deafening response: insults, a well-swung broom, childish screeching, and sonorous fartings. The paramour was torn between an imperious desire to stand up for her rights and the demands upon her to become temporarily invisible, uprooted by the arrival of Teodora Vencejos and bundled off to the opposite side of town. And with her, her father, her mother, her younger children, her new dresses and shoes, her kitchen utensils, and her latest pregnancy. Galaor had bought her a house down by the river, with a small piece of land, a patio, a chicken house, and a raised sidewalk. He had even presented her with a brand-new Singer sewing machine, a color television, and a mirrored, double-door armoire. "Big deal!" she protested. The house wasn't suitable for her. It lacked elegance, prestige, eminence. She wanted to stay forever in the Hotel Ramona. To be owner, señora, respected mother, on the Calle de las Camelias.

"I won't go!" she screamed. "Not now! I've been here for three years, and I don't feel like moving now. I'm four months pregnant. This is my place. Galaor Ucrós, you are my husband."

Drifting up from her dream, Teodora could be heard murmuring to herself. "I wonder where Dr. Amiel is? Where? I wonder if he's happy and in good health? Does he have a wife?"

How much she would have enjoyed talking with him, confiding her anguish to him, asking his forgiveness for not having listened when he tried to tell her about the order, the symmetry, the propriety of things. Now nothing would ever be as it had been, she could never again meet his eyes, nor would her life ever be the same.

"Anything going smoothly is going smoothly," the doctor had said. "It's never a good idea to throw a monkey wrench into the gears of routine. Husbands who come home a day earlier than they planned are the ones who find their wives in bed with the fruit seller or the skinny guy from behind the neighborhood bar. But, if you keep to a plan . . . "

What Teodora could not hear were the words Visitación Palomino was directing to the wife of Alí Sufyan.

"Teodora is very far away from us. Too far. It is almost impossible for me to reach her with my humble knowledge. We must follow the remedy prescribed by the Goddess."

"What remedy?" asked Zulema.

"The universal medicine. Love."

"Love? With whom? Her husband has a lover. It's a well-known secret that he prefers other women to her."

"Love before or after the kiss?" Doña Argenis was nervously twisting the tail of her imported blouse.

"Before. Teodora has slept far too long. And the kiss comes at the end of the road. That is, if she is able to return safely."

"Who can the man be?" Zulema observed the sleeping woman, disconsolate.

"That man is my son, Perucho." Maternal devotion overcame Argenis Cervera's embarrassment. "I believe he has never had a woman, because of his voice, so unfortunate in such a big man. He doesn't want anyone to make fun of him, and he's miserable. To date, we don't know of any sweetheart, or any, shall we say, cavorting he's done. Making love to Teodora would do wonders for him."

"And what if he has misgivings?" Zulema wanted to be sure of their choice.

"We won't let that happen. We will give him some apple juice with opium drops, and he will never know whether he had hallucinations, a wet dream, or an overactive imagination. Is he in love?"

"I don't think so. My son has never been very lucky."

"Better and better." Luminosa was scurrying around lashing the air with hemlock and artemesia branches. "Nothing more healthful than first love."

"When?" Doña Argenis inquired cautiously.

"This very night. We must hurry, or Teodora will be lost in the deepest confines of oblivion."

All the better, as Zulema Sufyan had said. For once, fate was smiling. Perucho Cervera, who slept in the adjoining room to be sure that Teodora did not hurt herself when she was walking in her sleep, and who had stayed by her side through difficult nights, agreed to drink an entire jug containing the "water of life." As Doña Argenis herself had assured him, it was a drink that would help dissipate the energy field floating around Teodora's bed and forming pyramidal walls that did not allow her friends to communicate with her or bring her back to the real world.

Meanwhile, Teodora, in her wandering over the rough terrain of the past, was making the frenzied preparations demanded by her visit to Real del Marqués. As she had at other times, she had announced her trip several weeks in advance and was enjoying the delicious wait. Except that her spirit was at the edge of, and at the same time far away from, those familiar activities. What was going on? She saw Galaor running frantically up one street and down another, trying to reduce his enormous belly, while Demetria and Esmaracola, poor Cinderellas, were trying to force bunions and calluses into new shoes, after having gone for two or three years in sandals: bare heels, no sweaty hose. They, too, rejected elegance, they preferred loose cotton shirts, faded jeans, the dresses printed with huge flowers they bought in the open-air market. With Clavel's compliance, the expensive clothing Teodora sent was sold at a carnival price or swapped for lottery tickets. For La Quintanilla hoped for sudden wealth, in order to be able to hack into little pieces the bonds that chained her family to the despised Teodora.

Later, dreaming, dreaming, as if she were watching a movie of her past life, Teodora relished the deceptive happiness she had experienced during former brief stays in Colombia, when she had soaked in the odors of her native soil. Galaor and the two divinely dressed girls waiting for her in the airport, accompanied by a band playing songs straight from the heart.

> *I'm gonna build*
> *a castle in the air,*
> *somewhere, only for you.*

And, under an arch of flowers, the triumphal entry into the Hotel Ramona, closed to the public but bubbling with the fiesta that lasted the two weeks of her stay. Happy evenings when she handed out gifts to her friends and in return received turnovers, fried pies, and the sweets that during her exile had made her nostalgia all the more poignant: yam, *papayuela*, guava sponge cake, sliced *icaco* and *limón*. Galaor played the piano—barcaroles, sonatas, and minuets—dedicating them to his wife with tenderest smiles. Demetria and Esmaracola showed off their glowing talents and sang heartfelt duets.

> *Knowing you*
> *would come back soon,*
> *roses released*
> *their sweet perfume. . . .*

And at a given moment, Doña Argenis Cervera served white rum, whisky, and piña coladas, while the adults danced to old songs sung by Leo Marini. Galaor's leg parted her thighs, and she felt hot and cold, fear and joy, because the hour of love was calling, and the neighbors, as they said good-bye, argued over the privilege of putting up Demetria and Esmaracola.

Teodora loved and feared the hour of love. Lying for long hours beneath sheets perfumed with verbena and jasmine, she listened to the cooing of the doves. The other cooing, the soft words of Galaor, held the true dimensions of her life. The fine lips beneath the precious mustache pleasurefully followed the line of her shoulders, armpits, hips, pubis; his warm hands squeezed the marrow from her bones. Teodora thought she would die of desire and eagerness, so near the moment of yielding she had awaited for so long. But no! The famous golden rod, celebrated in other days by party girls and the purported nieces of Leocadia Payares, wilted just as it was slipping toward the oven kindled into a volcano. Weeping, distraught, Galaor reinforced the phrase that rakes and carousers had used to label Teodora's frustration: "My husband always leaves me hungry . . . "

Which was absolutely true. Sis boom bah, in seconds the vaunted apparatus faded from carrot to radish to an innocent lad's tiny bud. And no way around it. Bud it remained, to the embarrassment and shame of its owner. No matter that Galaor stuffed himself with seafood and powerful tonics prescribed by his physician or put himself on a diet of palm-tree fruit boiled in wine or *borojó* juice. The aforementioned object did not lift its head. As wicked tongues reported, it had been done in by Clavel's voraciousness. And as a small town is no different from the halls of Hades, Ucrós's misfortunes stirred civic imagination and creativity. Not only did sales of oysters and fried fish skyrocket. At the cool-drink stands, they blended concoctions called Potency, Boxer, and Beloved Woman, in which egg yolks, royal bee jelly and pollen, algae, and Chinese roots were added to the juice of an orange. Visitación Palomino could not keep up with the orders for ceviches—*chipichipi*, sea bass, and sierra boiled in lemon and Tres Esquinas rum—for the loafers at the American Bar. The market suppliers sent to the peninsula of La Guajira for iguana eggs, turtle and manatee meat, guaranteed to stir the fires of love, according to people who knew. The fact was that Galaor's impotence offended local pride. Many a man would have taken his place in those marital duties in which the previously alluded-to party did not score a goal or was checkmated.

Teodora—sleeping—still believed in her husband and attributed his failures to her repeated absences and once again committed the slip of asking Luminosa's advice. And did so aloud.

"What can I do? Ask María Lionza. What . . . ?"

"Do about what? About who?"

"It's Galaor."

"What's his trouble?"

"Lovesickness, and a weak reed."

"Don't worry. I'll take care of it."

"No doubt about it," said Luminosa. "The Goddess approves of our idea."

Half sleeping, half awake, stupefied, and as if he were living a story in the *Thousand and One Nights*, Perucho Cervera was led by Zulema and Luminosa to the sweat-moist bed where Teodora Vencejos lay moaning and sighing for a passion that had never been satisfied. The fire that was devouring her could not distinguish between a man's and a boy's body. And young Cervera was right there! Healthy, strong, eager—and until that night innocent of touching a woman's breast.

Even better, it was a Friday night. On the outskirts of Real del Marqués, the cumbiamba drums were warming up. Along the river, girls were running toward the night's celebrations. In the improvised spa, tourists heard trumpets and accordions and danced their versions of merengues, salsa, vallenatos. The rock music that shook the foundations of the Residencias Argenis—the last word in modernity!—masked Teodora's delirious cries.

THE DISCIPLE

To get married without a single centavo, credit in shops, or prospect of work is not a good idea. Teodora began to have terrible headaches in the face of such worry. What to do? And how to do it? The only solution to all their ills—Galaor judiciously outlined to her—was to sell the house and with that money open a catering business in Barranquilla. Teodora would work in the kitchen, and he, still confident of his appeal, would attract an elegant clientele. They would become famous, preparing exquisite menus for weddings and other celebrations. Within a few months they would have the whole city in their pockets.

"So let's get married now in a civil ceremony and later on as God decrees. You hear me?"

"Yes, my love, I hear you."

Teodora's head was pounding; she could not get anything out but "Yes, my love," and "Whatever you say, my love." Nevertheless, she believed in the seventh heaven she shared with Galaor during his habitual siesta in his hammock, legs intertwined, his masculine hand, when Teodora pretended to sleep, lightly resting upon her moist dahlia or awarding dancing caresses to breasts through a dress thin from laundering.

"Are you awake?"

"Yes, my love."

"Shall we sell the house, then?"

"Whatever you say, my love."

But just as they were ready to put up the For Sale sign, the emissaries of Dr. Amiel showed up. They had with them a briefcase filled with past-due drafts and bills signed by Teodora, along with all the IOUs Galaor Ucrós had sprayed through hotels, motels, bars, rooms-by-the-hour, roadhouses, billiard parlors, and other, unexpected, places like ice cream stands, dairies, and snow-cone wagons. The debts the two of them had contracted greatly surpassed the value of the property, and the seizure itself would not even cover the debts left by the departed Doña Ramonita. As for other solutions, Don Martiniano Vencejos had tied up the properties that composed the rest of the patrimony so they could not be touched.

As if following their example, close friends became emboldened to collect favors they had done Teodora, some so small she did not remember them. Buttonholes and hems stitched by Roseta; tamales cooked by Visitación; ridiculous sums for a pound of salt or three sticks of cinnamon charged at the Cerveras' shop. Alí Sufyan, always so devoted, brought up an item of lingerie Teodora had needed during the period of mourning for Doña Ramonita, when la Quintanilla had appeared as the last person to offer her sympathies and then taken possession of Galaor.

Overwhelmed, Teodora went to consult with Luminosa Palomino, the only person in all of Real del Marqués she dared asked for a kindness or credit. On that occasion the priestess of María Lionza had lit a candle stub and read the trembling flame.

"A man is waiting for you across the sea. The stars are traveling backward."

"A man? I already have the best man of all. And what do the stars have against me? What did I do to them? And what about love?"

"Love? That depends on you."

"I don't understand anything."

"Try to understand."

"And what about my marriage?"

Luminosa moistened her fingers with saliva and snuffed the guttering flame that had turned a smoky cobalt blue.

"I didn't see anything. I couldn't see it."

"I'm getting married, anyway."

"That's your affair."

"And money?"

"With the sweat of your brow, and other sweat. That's how you will earn it."

Because of the desperate circumstances, the wedding was organized with great haste. Dr. Amiel's emissaries prepared to carry out the legal seizure and were fiercely tightening the tourniquet. Teodora and Galaor had to act first and beat them to the draw.

"Amiel would not dare humiliate my señora, my wedded wife," said Galaor to console his bride.

The dress was lent to Teodora by Hada Reales, a sylph in her day (moved at the last hour by her love, and behind the backs of the Cerveras), and was scandalously tight on Teodora. The satin all too readily revealed dark nipples, rounded tummy, unshaven pubis, and, what was most absurd, the frenetic activity of the moths, literally maddened with hunger at the contact with warm human skin, that minute by minute were chomping into laces, cotton, passementerie, featherstitch embroidery, and French knots, gobbling up all the ties, straps, and threads that secured the elastic, even as Teodora was climbing the steps to the courthouse with a bouquet of small *cecilia* roses in her hands. It leapt to the eye that she was fidgety—as if, a little early, Hot Hands Galaor had been tickling her underarms, thighs, backs of her knees, and hollow of her throat, even the shell of her ears, knowingly perfumed by Luminosa Palomino, who at Teodora's pleading had agreed to bathe and dress her.

"What kind of wedding is this," squawked the gawkers. "The bride is giggling so hard she's about to pee."

After she had signed the certificate, spoken her "Yes," taken the arm of her brand-new husband, no doubt remained. The wife-of-a-moment had no shame! She was wearing nothing, but nothing, under the nuptial satin. The moths' deranged appetite for cotton had affected their cells, and they began to devour one another beneath the borrowed dress—to the delight of Hada Reales, whom a wholesale manufacturer of rosaries and santos had left standing at the altar—like the fabled sweethearts of Barranca—when he found out what kind of place she worked in. This was her opportunity. To burn the dress and put an end to that reputation of having been left "all dolled up and nowhere to go."

"Nothing, and no one, will ever separate us," said Teodora as she kissed her husband on their return to Real del Marqués—on a city bus, since there wasn't enough money to rent a taxi. "I will be with you forever and ever!"

Restrained by passion and overwhelming pride, clinging to Galaor's arm, Teodora walked up Calle de las Camelias to live her first day of love—without party, congratulations, champagne, or rice. She wanted only to savor a simple slice of cake, share a small glass of sweet wine and her intense happiness. Right at the door of the house, however, sat a huge box the size of a refrigerator, wrapped in silver paper and tied with a red bow. Its contents were, like everything in Real del Marqués, an open secret. And half the town, in small clusters, necks craned, was strolling up and down the street with a distracted air. It is clear that no one thought to warn Teodora of the danger that lay in wait for her. Well, not exactly no one. Peruchito Cervera tried to prevent her from accepting the fateful bundle, hanging from the drapery and ruching of her gown.

"Don't touch it! The boogeyman's inside," he blubbered, but the euphoric girl did not heed his warning. How could she scorn a gift! And besides, Galaor, who cordially detested Peruchito, had no hesitation about driving him away with a few surreptitious cracks on the head.

What could it be? Teodora vacillated before taking that poisonous present into the house, observed from the next corner by Clavel Quintanilla, the grim incarnation of vengeance. Vindictive, enraged, she had decided to create an eternal nuisance for her rival by sending her the daughters she had had by Galaor.

"Why didn't you prevent that marriage?" her friends asked her. "Ucrós has been talking about marrying for quite a while. You knew about it."

"I never thought the idiot would be so stupid."

"He must be in love," interjected Doña Argenis Cervera.

"Love, schmove," Clavel shrieked. "He was forced into it! But he isn't going to get to enjoy the icing. I'm pregnant again."

The girls, Esmaracola, four, and Demetria, a year and a half, released from the gift-wrapped box, unleashed a tantrum that lasted through the wedding night, with plenty left over for the following days. Teodora spent the hours of passion Galaor Ucrós had promised in cleaning up wet and dirty diapers, runny noses, spilled milk, and half-chewed food. All Galaor had to do was try to give her a kiss, a nibble, slip off to bed with her, and the howling and yowling would break out anew. The screaming justified Herod's edict, and the billiards players in the American Bar, who stationed spies around the clock to establish the moment Galaor's cue made its first carom shot, were losing bets hand over fist.

Padre Imeldo Villamarín, Alí Sufyan, and the lawyer Catón Nieto intervened when the girls began to call Teodora Mami. A Mami that broadcast "me-mes" in every direction. Mami, I want my sweeties. Mami, I want to go with my Papi. Mami, I want my titty, my bath, my 'tatoes, my milk. Fruitlessly, the harried couple searched for La Quintanilla. The fact was that the paramour was taking her revenge. Party, party. Hair, décolletage, kohl-lined eyes complimented by silks, necklaces, earrings, and brilliant makeup. She bathed in lavender- and patchouli-scented water and danced her way through all the *verbenas* on the Atlantic coast. Men fought to dance with the woman in the short, skin-tight skirt.

The worst of it was that Teodora felt sorry for the abandoned girls. And she also saw Galaor as a victim. If that soulless, perverse woman treated her two little girls so badly, what mightn't she do to an innocent, weak young man, an orphan to boot? Well, all right. She was capable, strong, and the daughter of Don Martiniano Vencejos. She had been raised by a virtuous, thrifty madrina. She would have time enough to enjoy her honeymoon; she had her whole future before her. To be a mother first did not bother her. Only Galaor's attitude did. He was sad, disconsolate. It didn't help to berate him. Of course, she realized that he visited the American Bar and returned in the early morning in a haze of rum or beer. The little girls demanded attention and care through the night. And when Teodora could draw a breath, and begged Galaor, "Come over here, hug me," he could barely keep his eyes open because of fatigue, all-night carousing, and self-pity.

"I can't today. Give me a little time."

Time was what ran out first. Two weeks after the marriage ceremony was performed, Dr. Amiel's emissaries decided to fulfill the threat of seizure. Accompanied by Catón Nieto, a clerk of the court, an assessor, and two moving vans, they began at dawn one Monday to do their job. Two movers carried out wardrobes, tables, chairs, consoles, even kitchen odds and ends, plus the piano and mirrors, before the insatiable curiosity of most of Real del Marqués. Among the gatherers, particularly noticeable were the pernicious gamblers writing down the number of taborets, frying pans, kitchen stools, sling chairs, and potties, with the thought of betting the numbers and the lottery. Galaor Ucrós had left by the back door. The two girls, crawling around on the floor, were crying in operatic tones.

By midday the house was so empty that the last moths, spiders, and lizards had fled helter-skelter. Amiel's emissaries pretended to listen to Teodora's pleas and then, after having her sign a document—before witnesses—in which she agreed to work with and for the doctor until her debt was totally canceled, they ordered the movers to put the furniture and household goods back inside.

Relieved, Teodora pawned her wedding ring to buy milk, eggs, oats, rice, and meat. She begged Doña Argenis to "keep an eye" on poor Galaor, who had returned, contrite, to look after the children and the house. And as she said good-bye, like someone being led to the rack, she promised to return shortly. It would be only a short trip to Bogotá: a half hour from the Soledad airport to Eldorado Airport. Three or four days to arrange matters with the doctor. No more, no less.

Amiel, who at that time was organizing his European business affairs and happened to be passing through the country, demanded that she devote all her time to him.

"You have no right to refuse. Or argue with my conditions."

She was in his hands! With his habitual insolence and lack of Christian charity, he enumerated what he expected of Teodora. She listened attentively, quietly, swallowing her tears. She could have alleged coercion, disrespect, injury to the female sex, the breakup of the nuclear family, violation of human rights. But if she did not pay with her labor, her house would be auctioned off and nothing and no one would save her beloved husband and daughters from further humiliation. And it would be several years before she could touch the rest of her inheritance.

"All right, Doctor. I'll do whatever you say."

"You're not doing me a favor. You're obliged."

Amiel demanded that she take charge of baking cakes, distilling essences, preparing banquets, trying out new recipes. Not only did he want a model, a muse, a travel companion, and employee. He needed her twenty-four hours under the same roof with him.

Working out an accord was not easy. At Teodora's request, each function was spelled out, along with the accompanying scale of rewards. Ordinary work was covered under the labor laws of Spain, where they would be going—without including the cost of her travel in her debts. Precise terms were determined for other services. They had to set up a thick ledger with many headings, so that Teodora's debt would be reduced according to the speciality performed. Prices increased and decreased according to the day, the hour, and the moment. (It should not be overlooked that Teodora had inherited Don Martiniano's business sense and was also a disciple of Doña Ramonita Ucrós, née Céspedes.) The deductions began at a thousand pesetas, converted into Colombian pesos; they doubled or multiplied according to Amiel's requests, whether for work or inspiration. They varied with a kiss on the ankle, the calf, the back of the knee, or the thigh. Whether kisses included tongue, eyelashes, hands, or voice. Whether Teodora was caressed on the neck, knees, shoulders, or behind; whether she was nude, wearing a brassiere or seamed stockings. Whether beneath her apron, silk teddy, or leotard. Whether it was a Sunday or a holiday, and whether those holidays corresponded to religious or civil celebrations. Whether he wanted her wet with water or wine, her breasts and navel encircled with stars, flowers, or red circles. Whether he wanted to gaze at her through lace, veils, parasols, or a rain of streamers.

It was a broad, daunting agreement without parallel in the history of law or commerce. Teodora—pray God Galaor would never find out!—bowed to Amiel's most absurd caprices. Prices went up if they showered together, and differed for bathtub, bath salts, or showers of milk or sangria. The application of perfumes and lotions cost much more, and the same was true of cravings not formally recorded, for which Teodora collected immediately and in cash. The one thing she never allowed the doctor to take by storm was the rosy jewel box that belonged—sealed in its depths—to her spouse, her royal master and señor, even though she might allow Amiel's arrow to disport itself among the grooves of her ear or the lines of her neck. Even to caress her shoulders and breasts with spirited nocturnal expeditions at full gallop. Not always, no. Only when Amiel's creative delirium urgently demanded it.

It was an agreement intended to last a year, at the most two, as the doctor's fame as a great master chef, creator of essences, designer of lingerie was consolidated under one trademark formed by his initials—Manuel Amiel Orduz Rey—which when playfully entwined became the word AMOR. As the agreement stretched into five years, Teodora agreed to Galor's idea, that they transform the house into a modern hotel. Afterward, through one thing and another, whole winters and summers trickled away. The hotel was not blessed with good fortune. The girls had to attend the best schools. Expenses kept growing. Sooner or later, nevertheless, Teodora would be free to resume her ardent wedded life.

Two lustrums, three years, and six months later, Teodora Vencejos was still obsessed with her initial dream. If she had not lost thirty pounds, indulged a whim to visit her family, and traveled inopportunely (ignoring the prudent counsel of Dr. Amiel), perhaps her fate would have been different.

RAPTURES

From the time of his adolescence, Perucho Cervera had suffered from loss of sleep, appetite, and tranquillity. Mooning over women, he daily devoured long legs, rippling hips, fine ankles. From afar, he could smell a cinnamony, satiny, or pommerose skin. His eyes followed sweet sixteens, chaste Daughters of Mary, flirtatious girls, and widows with hungry breasts, without finding anyone who deigned to take him seriously after his first hello. As always, there was one exception to the rule: Roseta, the little seamstress. An exception he did not take into account because they had known each other since childhood, and her love would not count as a conquest.

At twenty-three, Pedro Amado Cervera was a tall, husky young man with compact muscles, narrow hips, enormous hands, and an arrogant profile. His liquid eyes and broad smile gleamed. He should have been able to woo all the girls of Real del Marqués and satisfy a gaggle of voluptuous lovers. Nature, however, had resolved to undermine its own desire for perfection. Pedro Amado Cervera possessed a flutelike voice, punctuated with cracks and tremolos, that moved listeners first to amazement and then disrespect. Not even the purported nieces of Leocadia Payares, in a constant cycle of renewal, had the courtesy to stifle their laughter when they listened to him.

"Bad through and through," as Teodora said.

To overcome this handicap, the Cerveras, husband and wife, had taken their son to the finest specialists. With no beneficial result. Psychologists, endocrinologists, audiologists could not locate the germ of the problem. The flaw developed during his growing years, they said, and the root of the disorder undoubtedly lay in some apparently normal but atrophied gland. God or chance might save Pedro Amado Cervera. They must have faith.

Except during one or two prolonged drunks, Perucho never went to Leocadia Payares's. And when he did, he acted like a movie tough. He swigged whiskey, stared at anyone who sat near him, paid generously, and left without so much as a "How black are your eyes!" to one of the hostesses. And, as a result, remained as virgin as his mother suspected.

So, then, this man who for years had languished over women, good girls and bad, was like a fish in water when introduced into Teodora's bed. Feeling another's flesh, heat, and undulations, his spring began to ping at the speed of a machine gun.

"*Ayyyy, madre mía!*" La Señora Ucrós's cries were equally rapid-fire.

The contest between two starving bodies made the very tree of life burst into leaf. She, wandering in the depths of her dream and he, sunk in a strange sleeping-waking; both in wingless, windless, boundless flight. So, toward dawn, when Perucho in one last chapter of the anthology encased his stiletto in the precious sheath, he ended—at long last!— Teodora's ever more rapid fall toward the abyss that separates oblivion from madness. He left it there, as lively as in its first outing but at rest, pleasuring in that shelter made almost, almost to his measure, yet never included among his dreamed-of havens.

The music in the spa had faded with the last glimmers of neon. Hotel staff, laborers, and tourists slept. Luminosa Palomino, Doña Argenis Cervera, and Zulema Sufyan, who were standing guard in the adjoining room, peered in, attracted by the sudden silence. And from the bewitching smile on Teodora's face, they realized that the situation was under control. She was on her way back from danger. They could see it in her gleaming hair, her skin, satiny as a tuberose, in a laugh she was laughing to herself, a kind of cooing: the cooing of the ringdove.

As the "water of life" was wearing off, and while Perucho

was still infused with the intense pleasure of possessing Teodora, the women guided him back to his bed, taking the trouble to dress him completely, to avoid arousing suspicions about what had happened.

"Now, more than ever, we need Dr. Amiel," said Luminosa. "The chance to find another virgin, near at hand, won't come around again."

There was no doubt María Lionza had allowed this union to take place without the participants' awareness, so that in the future their thoughts would conjure up neither nostalgia nor memory.

"What is it, son?"

Perucho had awakened, crucified with thirst, toward dawn. He did not even remember he had promised to summon Teodora if he saw her in his dreams.

"I'm happy, and I feel like crying, and I need to piss. All three things at once." Perucho's voice resounded in the room. Masculine, warm, deep.

"Are you all right?"

"Never better!"

Perucho was completely dressed, right down to his loafers. He leaped out of bed with a bound. It was as if the genie of grace and virility had suddenly bestowed his gifts upon him. He ran to the window and shouted an "Aaa-aaah-aahhh-ah" that awakened half the spa and had the profound resonance of all the "aaa-aah-eeeeahhh-aahhhs" bellowed by all the actors who portrayed Tarzan since film appropriated that Edgar Rice Burroughs character. Perucho rushed from the Residencias Argenis, bounded down the stairs four at a time, and after a cup-rattling "See you later, Mama," ran eagerly toward the house where Roseta Alvira lived. Suddenly he had felt the seamstress's eyes locked upon him, seen her skirt swing gently as she walked to church, desired those pale lips sipping cool guava and tamarind soft drinks. He imagined himself slowly removing her clothes.

She was a decent girl—not much rhumbaing and partying for her—a member of the Daughters of Mary who had secretly promised to die an old maid if Perucho Cervera did not come to claim her. Her behavior, therefore, evoked disapproval and rejection from residents around the plaza. Who would ever have guessed? Roseta Alvira, whom they had never known to have a sweetheart or boyfriend, snatched from her house in the early dawn, half-naked, with her shoes in her hand. Perucho had swept her up in his arms, without allowing her a single word. Milkmen, bakers, and women on their way to mass swore they had seen the girl make the V for Victory sign with her slender fingers. And, what was even more disgraceful, that public kidnapping—fostered by the victim—seemed to enjoy a certain complicity on the part of Padre Imeldo Villamarín. For when the ever-so-prudish Daughters of Mary came to the parish church to protest such undignified conduct, the priest seemed not a whit horrified.

"What do you want, then?" he asked. "Roseta has always been in love with Perucho, and he was not, by any stretch of the imagination, a white knight."

"It is an affront to the sisterhood," the girls alleged.

"Perucho Cervera is rich and clever, even though he has that tootely-flutely voice."

"They say now he talks like any good Christian."

"Even better. I will settle his accounts."

"She's seven years older."

"She knows what she's doing."

"Perucho has insulted the entire female sex of Real del Marqués."

"We shall order them to be married at a high mass, to redress their sins."

For eight days and eight nights, Perucho Cervera and Roseta Alvira barricaded themselves inside a motel on the coast road, at the end of which time Perucho appeared driving an open-bed truck carrying an orchestra playing dance rhythms. He hung the national flag in his bedroom window, and on his behalf three waiters served various liquors, while friends, relatives, tourists, idlers, produce sellers, and bookies toasted his fortune.

"When is the wedding?" his mother asked.

"No idea. It's in the hands of Teodora Vencejos."

Roseta Alvira had said Yes, Yes, Yes, and again Yes, she would be the wife of Pedro Amado Cervera. With one condition: Teodora must be matron of honor.

"Teodora," he tried to protest, "is in lalaland. I'm afraid she's never going to come out of that coma, or be free of ridicule and humiliation."

"It's my dream. If she attends the wedding, our marriage will be a happy one. We will have many children."

"What if she never wakes up?"

"Go look for Dr. Amiel. His kiss will wake her."

"There's no other way?"

"No."

Perucho Cervera had opportunities to make out with ten, twenty, a hundred women, if he wanted to. Ever since he bellowed his "Aaaaa-ah-aaah-ah" from the balcony of the Residencias Argenis, marriageable girls were sighing over him. Ever since the peripatetic party in the truck, girls were making eyes at him. But still behind his back he could hear the giggles of sweet sixteens, matrons, good girls and bad girls. He would not trade Roseta Alvira, not for the latest Miss Universe tied up in tissue paper and satin bows. And to please her, he was ready to move the world. In his position as a wealthy man who had no concept of the value of money, as Alí Sufyan did, or children to support, like Durango Berrío, Perucho Cervera did not need to rely on the telephone trail the Turk had followed without ever leaving town. He dreamed of spending a fortune, traveling through ports and capital cities and beaches and casinos, living the good life, wherever Dr. Amiel was devoting himself to squandering his own fortune. Amiel was throwing his money away on women he didn't give a fig for, spending days at the baccarat and roulette tables, entrusting his school and business to incompetent hands. Already several imitators were selling a lotion called Ardent that caused allergies and hives but never burst into flames. A group of Latin Americans had bombarded Spain, Andorra, and Portugal with gastritis-producing comestible panties and sugar condoms. In Germany, sunflower seeds were being promoted as *machaca* eggs. A catastrophe! If Amiel did not lift his head from the sand and resolve the problem, he would end up with nothing. His reputation and prestige destroyed forever.

Before he left, Perucho had consulted La Palomino, who, standing before a map of Europe and swinging a pendulum, had pointed the pearly fingernails of a fat right hand toward the places Amiel preferred: Biarritz, Saint-Jean-de-Luz, Cannes, Nice, San Sebastián. And Madrid.

"And how will I find him?"

"He will find you."

Trusting in the power of love, Luminosa began to adorn Teodora in flattering colors and jewels and trinkets: eardrops, bangles, rings set with rubies and garnets, because red is the color of desire and passion. White cotton and satin dresses to symbolize the wind and time that carry all changes with them. Around her neck she hung two amulets: amber to bring good luck and quartz to concentrate the positive energies of the cosmos. She braided Teodora's hair with sprays of laurel, rosemary, and verbena, because hope is the last thing to be lost. "After every winter, every cataclysm," she murmured into Teodora's ear, "nature is reborn."

Besides Luminosa, who was spending hours and hours concentrating on the person of Dr. Amiel, Doña Argenis, Zulema, Hada Reales, Roseta Alvira, and the wife of Durango Berrío worked unsparingly to attract him mentally. In so doing they did not eat or sleep enough, they forgot to button their blouses or respond to greetings.

Of course, without the women's being aware of it, the town was already alerted. Bets were flying furiously. Would Dr. Amiel come back? Would Teodora recover her reason? With a kiss or a honeysuckle? How would it happen? What day and what hour? Padre Imeldo Villamarín, who because of the restorative mud looked twenty years younger, spoke from the pulpit, denouncing the unworthy vice of gambling and the vile schemes being woven around a drowsing woman. The city, for its part, raised municipal taxes on games of chance and on bingo halls, because the lottery could not be touched; it was run by the state. Clavel Quintanilla, with a new son in her arms, had begun to fear for the future of her offspring and decided to resort to drastic measures. She'd had enough. She wanted Galaor as a husband, not a "Don Galaor Ucrós," and had determined to wreck the plans laid by Teodora Vencejos's friends. She hoped Teodora would drift in limbo for all eternity! That way she could be declared feebleminded, insane, incompetent. Galaor could put her in an asylum, and she, Clavel, could take charge of bringing him, once and for all, to his senses. The waiting period Don Martiniano Vencejos had imposed before his daughter could enjoy the body of her inheritance was almost up, and who would administer her wealth? Doña Clavel Quintanilla. For "Don" Galaor was not going to go through a fortune that, if justice was served, belonged to Demetria and Esmaracola.

For his part, Galaor Ucrós no longer found anything desirable in the current situation. In the long run, it was more pleasant to have a noble, hardworking, angelic wife who resided permanently outside the country. In those lost happy times, he had done whatever he wanted. Besides, he was bored with La Quintanilla, her airs, her eternal pregnancies. He missed the money and the sweetness Teodora contributed to his everyday life. Maybe, maybe, if she awakened, his luck would turn. It was worth a try. If he lost weight, curled his mustache, gave up carousing, and acted like a repentant and loving husband, the superstition about the kiss might just work. She would forgive him, and why not? He, Galaor Ucrós, was her enchanted prince.

A kiss of love. A tiny nibble . . . Hurry! Teodora must not see anyone else's face when she awakened. Let no opportunist win the game! He had right on his side, plus all legal claims. And he was, after all, an expert in the erotic arts. La Quintanilla could testify to that; the purported nieces of Leocadia Payares and other young ladies of Real del Marqués could as well. It was Teodora Vencejos's turn. He would make her enormously happy. Where would she find another man like him? She could only be very, but very, grateful that he was dedicating the rest of his precious life to her.

So, for different reasons, Galaor Ucrós and Clavel Quintanilla both hired a band of thugs to intercept Dr. Amiel and prevent him from setting foot in the Residencias Argenis. The paramour, while she found an accommodating lawyer and doctor who knew nothing of the antecedents of Teodora or of the word compassion. Galaor, with the hope of losing the pounds that would again turn him into a hell of man.

BLISS

Neither Pedro Amado Cervera nor Dr. Amiel suspected a plot when, five days later, they arrived in Real del Marqués. A strange coincidence, or the bewitched pendulum of Luminosa Palomino, had brought them together in the Barajas airport. Precisely as Perucho was hailing a taxi and the doctor was on his way to buy a round-trip ticket to Paris, where he was awaited by three anxious disciples. As his only luggage, he was carrying a large bottle of Aflame, since his mademoiselles had a yen to make love on a barge docked along the Seine, where through open hatchways they could be glimpsed in a resplendent aureole and be desired by hundreds of astonished men and—oh, bliss!— envied by countless women.

The vacation trip Cervera had planned was the shortest any tourist from Real del Marqués had ever taken. His promise to Roseta came first. In addition, he had realized that Amiel was facing a danger as grave as Teodora's. In the process of flitting from one woman to another, he was running the risk of contracting AIDS or, what was even worse, of burning out; he might lose his taste for a single love and turn to boys, or live at the mercy of a lunatic cock, a body without a soul. Which was how Perucho came to give up any thoughts of himself and to lose his one opportunity to know the Europe he had dreamed of as a desirable—although not uncommitted—bachelor.

The travelers had not announced the date of their return. They hadn't had time to do so. Half the town, nevertheless, recognized them as they drove into sight. They came as passengers in the new taxi of Durango Berrío, who was working just for the sport of it. He was bored at home and preferred to be where things were happening.

Dusk was falling, and lipstick-red brush strokes streaked the sky. The men drinking beer on the newly constructed terrace of the American Bar declared the following day—with or without the permission of the mayor—a holiday. No one would go to work. Many sent notes to their wives and lovers, asking to have dinner and breakfast delivered. Others ordered shad or *bocachica-sancocho* from Visitacion Palomino's inn. The streets were teeming with vendors peddling red sheets, water beds, lobster and pheasant patés, French champagne, enormous prawns, caviar, truffles, pickled octopus. Teodora Vencejos was right at the heart of it all:

Trees were heavy with flowers, money was flowing, the Real del Marquesians all felt the need to go forth and multiply. Calculations had to be made, numbers shifted; if eight signifies infinity, one and three evoke God, and sixty is perfect and consecrated.

Nervous, watched openly as well as by eyes that pretended not to see, Manuel Amiel got out of the taxi, walked with long strides up the ramp that joined Calle de las Camelias—now a tourist sector—with the road around the city, then along the terraces bordering the modern pools that held the swirling medicinal waters and mud deemed to be miraculous. Perucho Cervera and Durango Berrío followed behind, but not far enough to escape attack by a swarm of men in masks who had been lurking in the doorway of the Hotel Ramona. Some of whom had been hired by Galaor Ucrós and the remainder by La Quintanilla, each in the interest of individual goals. Cervera and Berrío, faithful to Teodora and the doctor but a little out of shape due to money and the good life, fought back tooth and claw! They were nine against three. The thugs were armed with blackjacks, brass knuckles, and sand-filled saps. Perucho, fortunately, was able to exercise his brand-new baritone, else no one would have lived to tell the story.

"Hoodlums! Assassins!"

Thanks to the alarm raised by the personnel of the Residencias Argenis, the thrashing did not reach cinematographic proportions. But harm had been done by the time the aggressors fled. Perucho Cervera, with a smashed nose, gathered up Dr. Amiel, assisted by Durango Berrío. Very slowly, they crossed the bridge over the large pool, looking like a segment of a Holy Week procession. In the Hotel Ramona, Clavel Quintanilla had double-locked the bedroom where Galaor was sleeping off his latest drunk; her daughters, Demetria and Esmaracola, were standing guard in case he woke up and tried to force open the door. And in the back room of Alí Sufyan's shop, Zulema Sufyan, frightened by all the commotion, began to feel her first contractions.

The blood of friendship reddened the entryway, the corridor, the stairs, dropping like seeds of the pomegranate. With their last ounce of strength, Durango and Perucho deposited Dr. Amiel, shoeless and half dead, upon the bed where Teodora lay moaning. "Kiss her, kiss her, for God's sake kissssss herrrr," they croaked, intoxicated by the aura of *marañones* and sleep Teodora exuded. No one in the Residencias Argenis was paying any attention to them now, since they had all hurried to the aid of La Sufyan.

Excited bettors, of course, came running from the ridge of the cemetery to the Plaza Mayor, from the river to the market and the highway and the American Bar. Kiss or honeysuckle? This, in short, was the wagering, five to one, double, triple, even odds. Asisclo Alandete, who had been summoned by Galaor Ucrós to wax his mustache, was the target of a pail of hot water and La Quintanilla's wrath.

"Lowborn! Scoundrel! Bastard! If you come anywhere near my husband, I'll kill you. Oh, I wish Teodora Vencejos would drop dead! You'll be in for it if you say one word to my Galaor!"

A bleeding, filthy Amiel, spitting and drooling, dangling from the grip of Perucho and Durango, deposited a kiss on Teodora's neck, then, with a great clatter, fell off the bed. Outside, people were lining up to enter the baths. The hours trickled by with the speed of molasses.

Smiling, Teodora emerged from her nebulous lethargy. Where was she? Who was she? What was she doing here? Three men were asleep at the foot of her bed. Dazed and sweating, she sat up, with a delicious tingling over all her body. But her delight evaporated at the sight of Amiel: ripped shirt, swollen lips, puffy eye, and no glasses.

"Doctor. Dr. Amiel, my beloved love." Tenderly, she began to kiss his naked feet, toenail by toenail, toe by precious toe.

Fearfully, she ripped his white smock to bind up his cuts and scrapes. At the touch of her hands and her delicate caresses, tissue, muscles, skin began to heal. As she was removing his clothing, she discovered the bottle of Aflame in his shirt pocket. And remembered she had never experienced the joys of that marvelous potion—not with Galaor, not with anyone. What a fool she had been!

"My sweet darling, my precious Dr. Amiel." For the first time in his life she stroked the chest, the face, the eyelids of that man she had always loved madly and desperately, with a love beyond time, jealousy, possessiveness, beyond love itself.

She could barely, oh so faintly, hear the doctor breathing. He was cold as death. But the pale flesh she rubbed with Aflame was, second by second, recovering its natural color. Even so, his heartbeats were faint and irregular. Teodora felt life seething within her, her breasts trembled with love and desire, she was mad for her Amiel! Without a second thought, enraptured, she began to explore, section by section, every meander and nook of that masculine fortress: thighs, knees, arms, groin. Now on her knees, she admired the sex bursting with shot and firepower, even though the owner was at the very door of the void.

"One day," she whispered, "you and I will be like Romeo and Juliet, Paul and Virginie, Abelard and Heloise, Catherine and Heathcliff, Efraín and María, Simón and Manuelita, Wagner and Cosima, Don Quixote and Dulcinea, Salvador and Gala, Guinevere and Lancelot. . . ."

"Like Napoleon and Josephine, Antony and Cleopatra." Amiel completed the list.

His eyelids fluttered open, and with a malicious smile lighting his honey-colored eyes, he began to grope for the perfect throne, the rose he had so long coveted.

"Made for each other," said Perucho, suddenly shaken awake by Durango.

"Amiel and Teodora," said the taxi driver, lighting a

cigar, for after hitting it big he smoked Cuban cigars, and in Teodora's aura his pain had evaporated.

Suddenly the room glowed in a cone of light, and a bluish ellipse enveloped the couple as Teodora rode the horn of the unicorn.

"I told you." Amiel burst into triumphant laughter. "I told you one day I'd make that bud of yours burst into bloom!"

Her ringdove cooed hungrily, so avid that it could not be satisfied until dawn. Perucho Cervera and Durango Berrío, weary from applauding, went off to have a whisky. By which time Zulema Sufyan was cradling in her arms the two most beautiful babies in Real del Marqués—along with a prostrate, devoted, thunderstruck husband.

Teodora, perfumed with rosemary and verbena, peered into the marvels of the future. The world was so vast! And in it were so many, many men! Delicate Japanese, handsome Greeks, exotic youths from the Philippines; there were fiery Mexican machos and amusing Madrileños. And blondes. God, the blondes, with blue eyes the color of grapes or for-get-me-nots. And blacks shiny as olives. And icons of gold. And all the fabulous males of her native land.

"You are sensational," she said, flooded by the proximity of maximum pleasure. "You are one of a kind!" While, eyes closed, she promised herself a world with silk sheets, incandescent revels, and lovers sweet as honeycomb.

THE COLOMBIAN
KITCHEN AND GARDEN,
ACCORDING TO FANNY

Ajiaco. A wonderful potage typical of the Bogotá plains, in which
three kinds of potatoes are mixed with chicken and corn—and
green peas if desired—and boiled slowly to make a rich, thick
golden soup. *Guascas,* the leaves of a small bush grown only on
those plains, give the *ajiaco* its very specific and peculiarly delicious flavor. The dish is served very hot with avocado, capers,
cream, and the *ají* (chili pepper) that gives it its name. *Ajiaco* is
now included on the menu of a very famous Paris restaurant.

Alfajores. A type of rolled cookie formed in pairs and held together by
fruit jelly or cream filling. Fanny's definition is "a kind of twin
roll with soft milk fudge (*arequipe*) in the middle."

Altamisa. Maidenwort, of the Artemisia family. The long, dandelion-
like yellow-green leaves alternate with clusters of small yellow
blossoms. In one of its worst transcriptions, *altamisa* becomes
mugwort.

Anamú. The leaves of this tree have the reputation of curing cancer and dissolving tumors. It is also widely used by doctors as a cure for tuberculosis. It has migrated from the herb stalls in the market to health-food stores.

Arepas. Corn griddlecakes, perhaps most similar to the tortilla. The dough, of maize, salt, and water, is patted into rounds; *arepas* are sometimes made with eggs, cheese, butter, and sugar. There are many varieties, and they are cooked or fried according to region. Their color ranges from white through yellow to brown. These corn cakes may be filled with spiced ground or shredded meat or with egg. The Antioquia *arepa* is plain, made only from corn and water.

Avena. A powdery oat product mixed with cold milk, sugar, and vanilla and not unlike the North American Ovaltine. In the warm regions of Colombia, *avena* is sold on the streets as a cooling drink.

Borojó. A round, brown fruit, extremely rich in free essential amino acids, from which a nutritious health juice is prepared. It has popular fame as an aphrodisiac.

Caña. Sugarcane. In Latin countries *caña* is sold on the street, cut into sections and crushed so one may suck out the sweetness.

Cañandonga. In English, the "drumstick" or "horseradish" tree *(Díos mío!).* The fruit is a dark brown pod divided into compartments containing blackish, slightly bitter, slightly sweet pulp. A favorite of children despite—or perhaps because of—its unpleasant odor.

Carabañola. Fried pie. These small, oval-shaped treats are made of *yuca* dough and filled with spiced ground meat, meat stew, or cheese.

Cariaquito morado. A small bush with verbenalike flowers, purple or white, with a sweet scent. The widely sold soap is purple. Young girls hope for it to bring good luck with their boyfriends.

Cayena. Not to be confused with cayenne pepper, which took its name from a pepper that flourished on an island in French Guiana— except, perhaps, in color: the flower of the *cayena* is the hibiscus.

Cecilias, or *cecilitas*. Small pink roses resembling the floribunda. They grow in small clusters, like small bouquets. Traditionally *cecilias* were pale pink, but now this beautiful rose, common in gardens in certain parts of Bogotá, is also cultivated in rose, yellow, and red.

Chicharrones. Chitlins. Crisply fried pork rind.

Chipichipi. A small, strongly flavored clam. Cooked with rice, it is popular as *arroz con chipichipi*. It is also served in soups, shellfish cocktails, and in many seafood recipes.

Chontadura. Fruit of a palm, *chontaduras* grow in grapelike clusters. During the process of maturation, the skin is green, orange, and tangerine. When ripe it is saffron, both outside and inside. It is usually boiled, peeled, and eaten sprinkled with salt, and in this form it is sold on the street. It can also be used in soups or juices. The fruit is very nutritious, high in protein and therefore considered to be an aphrodisiac.

Chuchuhuaza or *chuchuguaza*. A root credited to have aphrodisiac powers. Sold in markets or health-food stores.

Curuba. An oblong fruit tapered at each end, which when ripe has a silky green or yellow skin. It has a very distinctive flavor and is said to grow only in Colombia. The pulp has small brown seeds and is a very specific and special color—a delicate tangerine shade called, appropriately enough, *curuba*. It is delicious in juices and desserts. When beaten with sugar and milk and/or cream, *curuba* sherbet is an obligatory accompaniment to *ajiaco*.

Diosme. Diosma. Fragrant plant with very small, simple white flowers appearing individually at the end of sharp-leaved branches. It is very popular because people believe it brings money and good luck.

Dulces esponjosos. Any spongy dessert. An *esponjoso* may have the consistency of sponge cake or of whipped desserts like mousses. The texture of the dessert is filled with bubbles or holes. The test is that when touched with a spoon, the spoon does not sink into the mixture.

Espejuelo. Literally, "thin mirror." This candy made from fruit peel and has the consistency of a solidified Jell-O. It is shimmery and mirrorlike, the color of a ripe persimmon following the frost. The most common flavor of *espejuelo* is guayaba, and frequently *arequipe* (a soft, fudgelike chocolate) is sandwiched between two layers.

Esponjados. Unlike *dulces esponjosos, esponjados* may be either sweet or savory. They are made with beaten egg whites, condensed milk or cream, and gelatin. Fanny's own version uses thick fruit pulp and unflavored gelatin, without condensed milk. Sugar is added if needed. If preparing a chocolate *esponjado,* she uses cream.

Floripondio. This blossom in English is known as "thorn-apple," "purple stinkweed." (Why do some English names sound so much less inviting?) A narcotic brew may be prepared from the seeds. In most towns on the Colombian Caribbean coast, male homosexuals are called *floripondios.*

Fritanga. An assortment of fried foods. Usually beef, pork, assorted sausage (such as blood or Spanish sausage, *chorizo*), *yuca,* salted boiled potatoes or Creole fried potatoes, crisply fried pork rind (*chicharrón*), baked corn on the cob, and ripe baked plantain or fried green plantain—*patacones.* A *fritanga* is served with avocado or tomato slices sprinkled with salt and finely chopped fresh herbs. A *refajo* is obligatory, a beverage between soft drink and beer.

Galletas de ajonjolí. Sesame cookies.

Guanábana. In English, the "soursop" or "custard apple." The large fruit with slightly acid, white pulp composed of cottonlike flakes is used widely in soft drinks, candies, and preserves, especially in *marquesitas*—white or brown-and-white crystallized sugar decorated with one of the flakes in the center.

Icaco. A large bush that bears a white flower. The plum-sized fruit is whitish violet with rosy overtones. *Cascos de icaco*, slices shaped like orange segments, are served *almibarado*—in a heavy syrup.

Limonaria. Lemon grass. Pale green, sword-shaped grass that smells and tastes like lemon—at its most delicate. Used in teas.

Lulo. A fruit similar to the kiwi. The fuzzy skin is green when immature but when ripened is yellow or orangeish. The fruit has a pulpy core consisting of small dark seeds and emits a very strong scent. It is used to prepare juices and desserts and in some meat dishes.

Mamey. The dark exterior of this fruit is unprepossessing but when opened reveals a rich, honey brown pulp. The pits look like burnished ebony. It is eaten raw and when cooked is used for sorbets, syrups, and desserts.

Mamoncillo. Fruit of the genip tree. The flowers and the fruit grow in grapelike clusters. The fruit has a single seed, which can be eaten. The pulp, when ripe, is a beautiful color, like a pale mandarin orange; it, too, is edible but rather acidic. The skin is a smooth, intensely bright green.

Maracuyá. Passion fruit. This delicious fruit has a thick yellow skin, a strong, acid flavor, and a deep, orangeish pulp containing small black seeds similar to those of the *curuba. Maracuyá* is used in sweet juices and sometimes in spongy desserts. Colombianos love the strained juice—with water, sugar, and ice—as a splendid mix for rum, vodka, and various cocktails.

Marañones. Cashews. The body of the fruit, shaped like the nut meat but yellow or orange-red in color and many times larger in size, hangs from the fruit. The *marañon* has a strong flavor and aroma; the fruit is eaten when ripe, as is the nut, which is toasted or baked. In profile, the crescents face in opposing directions.

Matarraton. A tall, luxuriant tree with clusters of purple, rose, or white flowers. Its leaves are brewed to provide medicinal baths. If translated literally, it would be the "mouse-killer tree."

Merengones. Big baked meringues made in cake-sized layers and filled with fresh whipped cream and fresh fruit or soft chocolate fudge. Guanábana, raw fig, and strawberry *merengones* are Colombian favorites.

Merengues. Ordinary baked meringues. In size, between *merengones* and *suspiros.*

Mojarra. A marine fish not unlike sea bass. The oval body of the *mojarra* is covered with silver, blue, or yellow scales ornamented with black dots. This is a very tasty fish, usually served fried and accompanied with white rice, onion, tomato, and *yuca.* When used in *sancocho,* it is first fried.

Mondongo. Tripe stew. Spicy soup made of stripped and cleaned tripe, sliced potatoes and carrots, green peas, and pork.

Ñame. The edible, tuberous root of the yam, also used as the base of a very special custard dessert. On the Colombian coast it is an ingredient of *sancocho* and in purée form is called *mote.*

Níspero. Medlar fruit. A small, full-leafed tree with large pink or white flowers. The apple-shaped, light brown fruit is rather acid and ripens most quickly after a frost. Eaten fresh but also used for preserves and sweets. The seeds are thought to dissolve gallstones.

Panela. In most Latin American markets, brown sugar is sold in small compact loaves, *panelas.*

Panelita de leche. Milk candy. Related to a kind of blancmange. Sold in solid little squares.

Panochas. Large, round, dark cookies made from wheat flour and sugar, *panela,* or molasses. They are sold on the street and are perhaps the most common Colombian cookie.

Papas al ajillo. Peeled and sliced potatoes baked with butter and garlic. They may be sprinkled with parsley.

Papayuela. A small, oval papaya, with soft pulp and small brown seeds. When ripe it has green or yellow skin and is delicious in syrups for desserts. It is used as a medicine for bronchial infections.

Patacones. Fried, crushed plantain slices. The green plantain is cut into wheel-shaped pieces and fried, crushed with a stone or wood tool, and fried a second time. This Colombian treat takes its name from the gold doubloons called *patacones.* They are eaten with salt and are a feature of a *fritanga* platter.

Platanitos pícaros. Sounds like "scampish plantains." A dessert made from ripe plantains cooked in a syrup of sugar or *panela* and clove. *Pícaro* means spicy, all right, but usually in the rouguish or sexy sense.

Polvorones. Very similar to sandies. According to Fanny, they are small balls made from wheat flour. In Colombia they are made of butter or margarine, vanilla, nutmeg, cinnamon, and clove. They have a sandy texture and when bitten into shed something like *polvo,* "dust." Hence the name.

Pomarrosa. Pommerose, rose apple. This tree with particularly beautiful foliage bears a fruit with porcelainlike skin. The fruit exudes a very sweet, roselike fragrance. In Colombia, extremely naive people, or objects, are called *pomarrosas.*

Posta negra. A kind of rolled roast, the "black" in its name derives from the darkening effect of the *adobo,* or sauce, in which the roast is marinated. The *adobo* consists primarily of crushed tomatoes, onion, and garlic, with butter. The roast is sautéed in oil or butter and then cooked, tightly covered, over a slow flame.

Rollitas con queso. Long fingers of cheese—sometimes with raisins and honey added—wrapped in pastry dough and fried in very hot fat. They tend to burst but are delicious served with tea or coffee or at cocktail time. They are also called Olaya fingers.

Sancocho. The national dish of Colombia. A stew with many variations. Among other ingredients, it may contain pieces of chicken, cooked or salted beef, pig, or all of them, as well as fish, potatoes, *yuca*, chunks of corn on the cob, ripe or green plantains, and numerous spices and herbs.

Suspiros. Literally, "sighs." Small swirls of baked meringue served as candies or treats.

Yuca. Yucca, cassava, or manioc. The Spanish *yuca* is deceiving, for this is not the familiar flowering succulent of the North American Southwest but, rather, a tuber from which a starch is derived that serves as a staple of tropical diets. The roots resemble sweet potatoes. Its most familiar manifestation on non-Latin tables may be in the form of tapioca. *Yuca* is a must in the popular Colombian dish called *sancocho.*